SIN CITY HOMICIDE

A Thriller
By

VICTOR METHOS

Copyright 2012 Victor Methos
Kindle Edition
License Statement

Please note that this is a work of fiction. Any similarity to persons, living or dead, is purely coincidental. All events in this work are purely from the imagination of the author and are not intended to signify, represent, or reenact any event in actual fact.

1

Jon Stanton tore up his palms as he tried to leap over the
barbed wire fence.

He fell back in pain as the blood flowed. Looking up, he
could see the figure of a man wearing a jacket and baseball cap
on the other side of the fence. He stopped momentarily, turned
to him, and almost politely bowed his head before sprinting
again.

Stanton jumped to his feet and took off his jacket. He threw
it over the barbed wire and jumped up onto it, using his legs to
push himself over before letting himself fall to the pavement on
the other side.

Dashing through the alley, he spotted a stack of garbage cans
next to a dumpster. He pulled out his .45 caliber Desert Eagle
and spun around to the other side of the dumpster. No one was
behind it.

Stanton ran into the dark street. It was well past midnight,
and few cars were out so late on a Tuesday night. He heard
a crash across the street, where the figure was kicking in the
flimsy door of an apartment building.

Stanton sprinted over and held up his weapon as he entered
the building. The light-blue carpets were worn, and the walls
were stained. On his left, stairs led up to the other floors, and
a second stairway to his right led down to what looked like a
laundry room and the entrance to the parking garage.

Loud thoughts ran through his mind. Indian gurus called a

mind that couldn't quiet itself the *wild monkey*. He closed his eyes and focused on his breathing, counting to ten in his head until his mind was calm. His sense of hearing was keen, but he couldn't hear anything now. The building creaked and settled in for the night, but he couldn't discern anything out of the ordinary.

Stanton stepped gingerly down the stairs, remaining as quiet as possible. Then he heard a mumble from the floor above, hardly lasting more than a moment. But he had heard that sound before and knew instinctively what it was: a muffled scream.

He bounded up the stairs two at a time. On the second floor, with his weapon in front of him, he went slowly from door to door, listening. As he got to the end of the hallway, he looked toward the last apartment on the right. The lights were off, but the blue light of a television flickered under the door. The sound was turned completely off.

Stanton held his breath and said a quick prayer. He lifted his heel and bashed it into the door just underneath the doorknob. The door flew open and slammed into the wall as splinters rained to the floor.

In the living room stood Juan Roberto Gonzalez, holding a .32 caliber revolver to the head of a young girl, no more than twenty.

"I'll kill her," he shouted. "Back off. Back off!"

"What do you want?" Stanton asked, his weapon aimed at the man's head. Every time he had a clear shot, Juan pulled the girl up just a little farther.

"I wanna car. Ya hear?"

"The whole state's looking for you, Juan. Where are you going to go? They won't let you cross the border. They'll put a bullet in your head before they let that happen."

"Fine. She got a baby, too. I'm a pop her and then the baby and then myself. How's that, *puto*?"

Stanton lowered his weapon. "You win." He pulled out his keys. "You can take my car, but leave the girl."

"No way. She comin' with me."

"Okay, but leave the baby."

He was quiet a second and then nodded. Stanton threw the keys on the floor between them and began to back out of the apartment, holding his hands high, his weapon dangling loosely in his right hand.

There were moments, he knew, when a person could see the future. Not fortune telling—he didn't believe in that—but just moments where the outcome was certain, where nothing could change what was about to occur. He saw Juan's eyes go to the keys. That was such a moment.

His hand tightened over his Desert Eagle, and he lowered it to shoulder height. Juan's eyes went wide as he saw the movement and began to raise his gun.

Stanton fired. The round went through the girl's shoulder and into Juan's throat. He stumbled back as the girl screamed. Blood poured out of him, down his shirt, and onto the floor. He made an awful gurgling sound as he sucked for breath, but none came. He collapsed onto his knees and fell to his side.

Despite his insistance that he hadn't been hurt badly enough to warrant the attention, Stanton sat in the back of the ambulance as a young paramedic performed a routine check and bandaged his hands. The kid noticed the burn scars on Stanton's neck.

"What happened?"

"Wasn't as lucky that time."

After the kid was convinced Stanton was fine, another detective informed Stanton that he would have to go down to the precinct the next day and provide a full statement about the shooting. The detective also took Stanton's sidearm. Stanton then got into his car and drove to the Scripps Hospital nearby. He went to the ER, where the young woman was being treated. He waited until the staff had cleared out before entering.

"How you feeling?" he asked.

"You? What you doin' here?"

"I just came to see if you were okay."

"I would be if you hadn't fucking shot me. I'm a sue your ass and the police. My uncle's a lawyer and says we got a case."

"Was he the first person you called?"

"What? Fuck you. You better—"

Stanton didn't wait to hear the rest. He turned and made his way out of the hospital. He sat down on a bench near the entrance and watched the moon for a long time. He had left instructions with one of the rookies to notify him of any news about Juan Gonzalez. Twenty minutes later, he got a text—Juan had survived. He would live, but he would be in the ICU for at least a week until he could have reconstructive surgery on his throat.

Stanton breathed a sigh of relief. He wouldn't be sleeping that night, but at least he could lie in bed and calm his thoughts. As he walked to his car, he saw a man in a suit carrying a briefcase enter the hospital with a younger man, who appeared to have just woken up. They were talking about what a great lawsuit they might have against the San Diego PD.

2

Stanton woke early and went surfing at Ocean Beach Park. Earlier that month, a couple had been canoeing not a hundred feet from shore when their canoe overturned. Only one body was recovered. He'd known them well. They had spent time together in the ocean, waiting for the waves to pick up. He had liked them, but realized he didn't remember their names. It bothered him a few moments, then he pushed it out of his mind.

After showering and dressing, Stanton dialed a number on his cell as he left his apartment on the eleventh floor of one of the poshest buildings in San Diego. He'd rented the place from an absentee landlord who had relocated to Florida. Stanton put a check in the mail every month, and the guy left him alone.

"Hello?" A female voice answered the call.

"Hey, Mel, it's me."

"Hey, you just missed them. They headed out to their friend James's house for a sleepover."

Stanton cringed. He had warned his ex-wife repeatedly that sleepovers weren't permitted. His sons, who were eleven and six, were too young, and he had seen far too much happen at sleepovers during his time as a Sex Crimes detective years ago. Too often, mothers wounded from marriages that had fallen apart unexpectedly fell victim to the charms of predators. These stepfathers and boyfriends sought victims wherever they could find them.

"I don't know how many times I can say this, Mel. How many times do we have to have this conversation?"

"If you don't like it, we can go to court and have the judge decide if sleepovers are okay. I had them growing up, and nothing happened, Jon. You need to relax."

Stanton exhaled and closed his eyes as he waited for the elevator. Not even a semblance of a relationship was left between them. His words carried no more weight than a stranger's.

"I gotta go. I'll call them tomorrow."

It was nearly ten o'clock when Stanton hopped onto the freeway and headed to the Northern Precinct. Traffic was light, and he listened to a Moby CD, skipping the songs that had lyrics. The day was turning out to be hotter than he'd expected, and he took his sports coat off at a stoplight, letting his badge dangle around his neck on a thin chain, a tactic he had picked up from Lieutenant Daniel Childs when Childs had been a detective. If he wore it around his neck, he was less likely to lose it. Few things were as humiliating for a police officer and it was a constant worry of his.

He pulled into Northern and parked. Uniforms were buzzing around like bees in a hive as he walked into the building.

The secretary at the front desk saw him and smiled. "How are you, Johnny baby?"

"Good, Candace. How's Jake?"

"He's getting bigger every day. Pretty soon he's gonna have to be potty trained."

"Well, don't go too hard on him. We tried to get Matty potty trained before two, and he got so scared of the toilet he wouldn't go into the bathroom until he was almost four."

"We got a video with Elmo. It's supposed to be the best thing out there, but we'll see how it goes. Um, did you see that email?"

"What email?"

"IAD's here to interview you."

"Yeah, I was in a shooting yesterday."

"Oh, no! You okay?"

"I'm fine. The perp's gonna live, too."

"Oh, just routine bullshit, then, huh? Well, they're waitin' for you in the interrogation room."

"Subtle. They couldn't do it in the lounge?"

She laughed. "Them boys are wound up so tight, I'm surprised they can walk with those sticks up their butts. Be careful with them, Johnny."

"Thanks."

Stanton walked down the hall, past the interrogation rooms, to his office. He placed his wallet and cell phone in his desk drawer before locking his office from the outside. Although it was a police precinct, thefts were reported every week.

He went down to a storage room at the back of the building, found the thermostat, and turned up the heat to one hundred degrees. Then he went out front, where he opened all the windows and closed all the vents. Then he went to the lounge and waited. He was willing to bet IAD would never take off their suit coats during an interview.

In about ten minutes, the building heated up enough to make him sweat. He found the open interrogation room, where two men were sitting on one side of the large gray table.

"Hi, I'm Jon Stanton. I'm here for an interview."

"Oh, yeah," a tall man with dyed black hair said as he rose. "Please, Detective, have a seat."

Stanton sat across from them. The other man was hefty with a round, cherubic face and balding hair that was gray at the temples. He was smiling widely and had his hands folded in front of him on the table. Sweat was pouring down his shining forehead.

"I'm Lieutenant Barkley, and this is Lieutenant Davis. I don't think we've met before."

"No, not since IAD got transferred to the administrative offices. I don't get down there at all."

"Well, this is a formal interview about the shooting of Mr. Gonzalez. You should know that we spoke with the victim in this case..." He flipped through his files. "A Ms. Vicky Guler. Would you like to read her statement?"

"No."

"Now, Jon," Lieutenant Davis said, "we're on your side. We just want the truth. Hell, I think this was a clean shot, and I'm embarrassed that we gotta even do this." He pulled out a hand-kerchief and wiped his face. "The more truthful you are with us, the sooner this will be over."

"You guys haven't read my file, have you?"

"What makes you say that?"

"I have some experience with IAD. If you'll pardon the insult, I don't have a lot of faith that you're on my side. Let's just do this and get it over with."

Barkley pulled out a digital recorder and hit record. He placed it on the table between them. "You don't mind, do you?"

"No."

Sweat was forming on Barkley's forehead as well, but mixed with the black dye in his hair, it looked like cola.

"Good. Ah, for the record, this is interview number one with Detective Jonathan Nephi Stanton, conducted by Emmett Barkley and Mark Davis of Internal Affairs Division. February twenty-two." He cleared his throat as he shuffled files and pulled out a couple sheets of paper. "Now, Detective, please tell us how you first made contact with Mr. Juan Gonzalez."

"Narcotics had gotten a tip from one of their CIs. They had been making controlled buys of heroin from Mr. Gonzalez for the past three weeks. One of the CIs who was making the buys said that when he went to the house for the pick-up, Mr. Gonzalez had a woman locked up in his bedroom. He asked the CI if he would like a 'go' with her. On the house."

"And this was a prostitute?" Davis interrupted.

"No, this was a mother of four who had been kidnapped in a mall parking lot. He'd had her chained to the bed frame for three days when the CI arrived. She had been brutally—"

"We don't need to go into specifics, Detective. So, you still haven't answered our question: how'd you come into contact with Gonzalez?"

Barkley wiped his forehead, leaving a black smear.

"The CI told his handler in Narc, and the detective informed Sex Crimes, who informed us. The victim's husband had been shot in the head during the kidnapping, and the case was active with Homicide. Sex Crimes and Homicide conducted a joint operation."

"What did that operation consist of?"

"We raided Mr. Gonzalez's home. We saved the victim, but Mr. Gonzalez jumped out of the back window and took off through the neighborhood."

"Was the back of the home not covered?"

"It was. The window was next to a tall tree. He jumped into it and then leapt into his neighbor's yard. By the time officers hopped the fence, he was already sprinting from yard to yard. We called for a chopper, but none were available at the time."

"So what'd you do?"

"I chased him on foot."

"You? By yourself, without backup?"

"Yes."

"Are you aware," Davis said, fanning himself with a file folder, "that protocol requires that an officer have assistance in this type of scenario? Especially with a suspect considered so highly dangerous?"

"Yes."

"And yet you chose to ignore it?"

"I chose to catch him rather than lose him. He had cash and connections. He would've fled to Mexico and we would've never seen him again."

"So what happened when you caught up with him?"

"He was in the girl's home, Vicky Guler, and he had her by the throat, with a .32 caliber revolver to her head. He threatened to shoot her and her baby, who was in the apartment. He was asking for a car. I pretended to give in and threw my car keys to him. When his attention was diverted, I fired."

"And you accidentally hit Ms. Guler?"

"It wasn't an accident."

"You shot her on purpose?" Barkley said incredulously.

"I had to. I knew the round would go through the fleshy part of her shoulder and wouldn't cause too much injury. I had to save her life. I made a call."

"And you stand by that call?"

"Yes."

Barkley shook his head. The black smear had spread down his forehead, and Davis noticed but didn't say anything.

"Thanks for your time, Detective. We'll be in touch."

Stanton left and went to the storage room to turn down the heat. He went back to the main floor, where he watched the two IAD officers leave the room, Barkley rubbing furiously at his head with a napkin. Neither had taken off their suit coats.

He went back to his office and collapsed into his chair, staring at the ceiling. Glancing to his right, he saw the files for his open cases: fifty-seven in total. His pile was higher than the other detectives' because he took the cases no one else wanted—the ones with no leads, no motives, and no suspects. The victims disappeared like ghosts but clung to life through him.

Stanton began going through his emails. The forty-one un-read messages were mostly departmental emails about policies, updates on cases, or notices for birthdays, retirements, new babies, and deaths. He scrolled down about halfway to a name he hadn't heard in a long time: Orson Hall. He opened the email.

Jon, long time, Brother. Please call me. I need your help desperately.
Assistant Sheriff Orson Hall,
Las Vegas Metro Police, Homicide Division

The "Las Vegas Metro Police" and "Homicide Division" weren't a tag on his email. He had typed them in. Orson was telling him something with that, but Stanton wasn't sure what. He was sure of one thing: the message was important. Stanton hit the speaker on his phone and dialed the number at the bottom of the email tag.

"This is Hall."

"Orson, this is Jon Stanton."

"Holy shit, Jon! How you been?"

"Good. How's Wendy and the kids?"

"They're great. Wendy went back to work 'bout eight months ago. It's making life a little easier on me."

"That's great. She was a nurse, wasn't she?"

"Yeah, ER. Good money in it. She makes more than me. How's Mel and the boys?"

"We divorced a while ago."

"Oh, wow. I'm sorry, man. I didn't know."

"It just wasn't meant to be, I guess. So, what's up?"

"Well, I got a little something here that I think I need your help on."

"What is it?" Stanton picked up his grip strengthener and began to squeeze in a slow rhythm.

"Rape-homicide. A couple. The guy's kind of a big shot in town, and I need some help."

"Have you called the feds?"

"FBI? You shitting me? They're ninety-nine percent terrorism now. If your perp's name isn't Omar or Muhammad, you're at the bottom of the list. Besides, to be totally honest—how long's it been since you been up here in Vegas?"

"At least five or six years."

"And you probably remember we were pretty ahead of the curve even then. A lot's changed, even since then. We got new labs and an expanded CSI unit, thanks to the TV show, I guess. Kind of a self-fulfilling prophecy. Everyone expected us to have the best, and so the higher-ups just fell in line. Anyway, my point is that I think we even got the labs in Quantico beat."

"Really?"

"Yeah, really. I'm not just blowing smoke, either. So, I don't need the feds for that. I need something else."

"What's that?"

"I need you, Jon."

"Orson—"

"I know, I know. You think I'm superstitious, don't you? But there's something to the way you think, Jon, that I haven't seen in other detectives. You know these fuckers inside and out. Call it a sixth sense or imagination or whatever. Harlow knows that.

That's why he recruited you for that bullshit Cold Case Unit of his."

Stanton grew uncomfortable and put his feet up on the desk in an attempt to force himself to relax. "I'm pretty swamped with my own cases right now."

"I hope you don't take this the wrong way, but I already spoke to the assistant chief over there. What's his name? Hu?"

"Chin Ho."

"Yeah, I spoke to him and we worked something out. He'd be willing to bring in another detective to cover for you while you come out here."

"How'd you convince him of that?"

"We got something over here you guys need—money. Money speaks louder than anything else."

"You're going to pay them to have me come out there?"

"We can talk about the details later, but you wouldn't just be working. I'm going to set you up in one of the nicest hotels out here. Anything you need, you tell us. You wanna fly your boys out on the weekends? It's done. You wanna drive around in a Ferrari while you're here? No problem."

"This guy was that important, huh?"

"More than you know."

"All right. I'll come take a look, but I gotta tie up a few loose ends."

"I'll book your flight now for Saturday, first-class. I really owe you one, Jon. I'm not kidding. You call in that favor whenever you need."

"I'm just taking a look at the evidence, Orson. I don't know if there's anything I can do."

"Well, whatever, just get on that plane. I'll feel better just having you out here."

Stanton ended the call and noticed Lieutenant Childs standing at the door with his arms crossed. He had built even more muscle over the past few months, and they bulged underneath his smooth, black skin.

"Old friend?" he asked.

"I did some consulting work for him when I was still a grad student. We've stayed in touch since then."

"All expenses-paid trip to Vegas? Sounds good to me."

"Maybe. If he's calling me and willing to shell out that kind of cash, it means he doesn't have any other options. If I can't help him right away, I'll be flying coach on the next plane back here."

3

By Friday, Stanton had passed his cases over to the detective brought in to cover for him. He was tall and lanky, with wrinkled suits and worn-out shoes, but he struck Stanton as honest and hardworking. After he had given him the last case, Stanton was notified that Assistant Chief Ho wanted to see him at the SDPD headquarters uptown before the day's end.

Stanton left the office around three o'clock to go surfing. He might be in Vegas for a while, and he hoped missing his morning ritual of being out on the waves wouldn't be too much for him. When he was married, every vacation they went on had to be near a beach, and Stanton hadn't left San Diego since the divorce. When he'd agreed to help Hall, he hadn't considered that it would mean taking a break from surfing.

The waves were mediocre, and he sat out on the water for a long time, lying flat with his stomach against the board. Letting his legs dangle in the waves, he let the surf push him back toward shore. The water was murky but the sun was bright, and there were few clouds. He caught a glimpse of a group of kids getting surfing lessons on the beach. He had tried to teach Matt and Jon Junior how to surf several times, but neither had been interested. They were obsessed with football because Melissa's boyfriend played for the Chargers. She had met him at the gym where she worked as a personal trainer. He'd heard through mutual friends that the relationship was serious.

Stanton paddled in softly, stood up when he was twenty feet

out, and walked back to the beach. He watched the kids for a while and instinctually scanned around for single men watching them as well. His pleasant thoughts were immediately followed by an unpleasant one of what others could be doing or thinking. His mind had few barriers, and thoughts, both pleasant and horrific, flooded his consciousness every second.

He went to the car and opened the passenger door to prevent prying eyes as he changed into jeans and a button-down shirt, then he hopped onto the interstate. He drove slowly, listening to the jazz station, until he pulled into the new SDPD headquarters's parking lot. He never ceased to be amazed how clean the grounds were kept considering his own precinct had recently developed a mouse problem. Several times, he had found droppings in his drawers and filing cabinets. Here, trees were planted in a pleasing arrangement, not too many and not too few. He had to sit in his car for a few minutes and prepare. A lot of his ghosts haunted that building.

When he finally got out of the car, he took his time getting to the front entrance. The layout was exactly the same as it had been the last time he was there, meeting with Ho about a case that had ended with him receiving second-degree burns over ten percent of his body. He nodded hello to a security guard at the front desk who didn't nod back, then went to the elevators and hit the button for the fifth floor.

His heart racing, Stanton stepped off the elevators and had to consciously calm himself. The map he didn't want to see was still posted. It was titled "Where in the World is Eli Sherman?" Sherman was his former partner, and he'd put two slugs into Stanton when Stanton discovered what Sherman had been hiding from him. In the nearly five years that had passed since Sherman escaped from custody, the map had filled with pushpins marking locations where Sherman had allegedly been spotted. There was currently no active search for him, just a spot on the FBI's Ten Most Wanted list.

"Jon," Ho said, walking up to him with a cup of coffee in hand, "how you been?"

"Good."

He noticed Stanton looking at the map. "Still gotta be weird, huh? Seeing Eli's name and knowing he's out there."

"That's one word for it. What is it you wanted, Chin?"

"Come on back to my office. I wanted to talk to you about something."

Stanton followed him down the hall. Ho swiped his badge at a thick door and it clicked open.

"You haven't been out here for some time," Ho said.

"No, not since you guys settled the lawsuit with Putnam's family."

"Oh, yeah, that pedophile that jumped off the building, right?"

Stanton knew Ho remembered, and it bothered him that the other man was so dismissive about it. "Yeah" was all he said.

"I know you didn't do anything wrong in that case, and the chief knew it, too. We were just sick of it in the papers all the time and the decision was made to settle."

They walked into his office, which was immaculate, and the smell of wood polish lingered in the air. Vivaldi was playing on the computer.

"Have a seat."

Stanton sat across from him and waited for Ho to close the windows on his computer before turning to him.

"Do you know why we're sending you to Las Vegas?" Ho asked.

"Orson promised you something. Either money or resources."

"Yeah, he did. They're cutting us in on their grant. Some county grant they have out there for law enforcement. Orson promised me and the chief that he could secure the grant for SDPD. It has to do with some forensics seminars. They're going to hold them here and sell tickets to law enforcement around the country. They get a grant to set it up and pay for the speakers. We're going to split the ticket sales. Should be pretty good for our reputation to host something like that, too." He took a sip of coffee. "The question I have for you is does he have that kind of juice? He's just an assistant sheriff."

"Orson's also the son-in-law of the mayor of Las Vegas. If he says he can do it, he probably can."

"Hm. Good to know. So how long you gonna be out there?"

"I don't know. I told him I'm just going to look at some evidence."

"Well, take as long as you need. We promised full cooperation."

"Fine. Anything else?"

He sipped his coffee, watching him intently. "You know, we used to be friends once."

"Once, Chin. Before you hung me out to dry on that Putnam suit. You offered me as a sacrifice so the county wouldn't have to pay for the lawsuit."

"It wasn't anything personal. It was a lot of money, Jon. We would have done it to any officer. Sometimes you gotta take one for the team."

"Is that all? I have to pack."

"Yeah, that's all. You're dismissed, Detective Stanton."

Stanton rose and began to walk out.

Ho said, "And Jon? Keep your nose clean out there. We need this money. Your suit still ended up costing the county, and we got a budget shortfall now. If this falls through, it's going to mean people's jobs."

Stanton saw the Rolex watch on Chin's wrist. "Nice watch."

He turned and walked out without looking back.

4

Bill James stood on the balcony of the top-floor suite of the Havana Hotel. The casino was directly below him, covered with a transparent dome, and he watched the people at the tables, letting the dealers slowly suck the life out of them. He looked out at the strip and watched the crowded sidewalks filled with families. He was in his sixties now and he remembered when Las Vegas was a place for men, where they came to get away from the family, the job, and life. Now it was a vacation spot accommodating the things men used to escape from.

"The times, they are a-changing," he mumbled under his breath.

"Sir?" said his assistant, Jaime.

"Yeah?"

"They're ready for you."

"Thanks."

He straightened his silk Armani tie and checked the gold cufflinks on his shirt before walking back into the suite. The top three suites were reserved for him. He kept one for himself as his home, one for any dignitaries or celebrities he wished to shower with special treatment, and one—this one—he had turned into a boardroom.

The board of directors of MJF Industries, the parent corporation of Havana Inc. and the true owners of the hotel and casino, had already gathered and were conversing quietly around the twenty-seat mahogany table. The twelve of them were all men of wealth and influence, and many of them—oddly enough, thought James—were extremely obese. With the kind of money they had, he figured they would have the best chefs and personal trainers.

James took his spot at the head, in front of the nameplate marking it as the chairman's seat. The CEO, Milton Henry, sat next to him, playing around on his phone, and the CFO, Raj Kamal, was on his other side. The board had asked that these two not be present, so James had made a point of having them here.

Half-eaten Iranian caviar and freshly made pastries were spread out on the table like leftovers from McDonald's. The board members began pulling out cigars and asking the assistants standing behind them for brandy.

"I think we're all accounted for," James said. "Jaime, stop taking minutes, would you? Thank you. So, we all know what we're here for. We've gone back and forth for the past three months, and it's decision time."

Cal Robertson, an older man with thick glasses and a ridiculous polka-dot bowtie, leaned forward through his cigar smoke. "Bill, we all agreed that we would sleep on this for the next quarter. Calling this meeting was unnecessary. I was in Boca Raton on this fabulous—"

"We can't sleep till next quarter, Cal. We need to decide now. This merger is going to secure the future of this casino. It's going to take us into the next century of entertainment."

"We're making a boatload of money as it is," Kevin Daugherty chimed in. "Why risk it on a venture that could go belly-up in weeks? Anyway, that's the way I see it. It's too much risk."

"We're in the business of risk," James said, "and we're at the point where we need to bet the house or go home." He turned to Raj. "What are the financials like?"

Raj cleared his throat, and an obvious tremor shook his hands as he began to speak. "Um, well, we've been losing market share the past three quarters to the bigger casinos. The, ah, gambling demographic has been decreasing over time, as we predicted it would in a bad economy. So people aren't gambling as much, and the ones who are, have been going to the casinos that give them better comps and are more family friendly, like the Mirage and MGM."

"How much money did we lose?" James asked.

"We've lost an average of sixty million per year for the last three years."

James looked out over the board for reactions, but he saw none. Some weren't even paying attention.

Cal said, "I just don't see the point. It'll turn around. It always does. All of us here are taken care of, and so is upper management. If some low-level shits have to lose their jobs, so be it. Let's just hang on and see what happens."

"What will happen is that we will go bankrupt, gentlemen. We can't wait. This merger with Sands Corp will change the playing field. Separately, let's be honest, we're mediocre casinos, but together, we could have the emerging gambling markets cornered. We'll establish ourselves as the gambling destination of the world."

Cal looked at his fellow board members. "We've talked about it, Bill. We're going to vote against it."

"Talked about it? When the hell did you talk about it? Where was I?"

"We're sorry, Bill. The answer's no."

The board members rose and filed out. James sat, incredulous, watching them as if he were watching aliens on a foreign planet. They were going to allow the company to crumble. They didn't care—it wasn't their baby.

Part of the trouble was that they didn't understand business. They saw the endeavor as a temporary fix, something they could use to make quick money and then abandon. They didn't care if they left anything behind because it wouldn't matter to them anymore. He saw it as something else entirely.

James turned to his bodyguard, Phil, who was standing behind him. James gestured for him to come over. He leaned down next to James.

"Cal has a mistress he's keeping in those condos over on Hollywood. You know where they are?"

Phil nodded.

"Go knock her around a little bit. Don't let anyone know it was you."

Phil left without a word. Milton and Raj sat looking down at the table, pretending they hadn't heard anything.

"Bad move?" James asked.

Milton shrugged. "It's just a mistress. Will he even care that much?"

"No, but it'll sure as hell ruin his day."

"Won't he retaliate?" Raj asked.

"I got nothing in my life for him to retaliate against. We got more pressing problems anyway. What do we do about the board?"

"They won't approve this, boss," Milton said. "There's no way."

"They're idiots," James said.

"No, they're cowards."

James held up his index finger as if a powerful idea had struck him. "You're right—they *are* cowards. How do we get them the necessary courage we're looking for?"

Raj said, "We need to make the alternative worse. It has to be more costly for them not to go through with the merger than to go through with it."

"And how do we do that?"

"I don't know yet."

James exhaled loudly and rubbed his head. He had a massive migraine, and he hadn't eaten yet.

"Think about it and get back to me."

The two men glanced at each other, rose, and left the room, leaving James alone. He leaned back in his chair and stared at the ceiling. He realized he no longer lived in the Las Vegas of his youth, the one where cheats were taken to the desert and forced to dig their own graves. There was a different set of rules at play now.

He pulled out a cigar from one of the silver cases on the table and lit it. He'd just ordered the beating of an innocent woman and hadn't given an order like that in a long time. He wondered if that was what he needed, what had been missing in his life. It was a chilling thought. He pushed it away as he sat puffing the cigar and looking out the floor-length windows to the streets below.

5

McCarran International Airport was packed with the weekend crowds when Stanton stepped off the plane and into the terminal. He walked down to the baggage claim and gathered his two gym bags. Being without his firearm felt odd, but he had already put in a request to Orson for a .45 Desert Eagle.

Outside the terminal, a man in a button-down shirt and sports coat held a sign that said, STANTON.

"I'm Jon Stanton."

"How's it goin'? Marty Scheffield. I'm with the police. Sheriff Hall's havin' me pick you up."

Marty took his bags and loaded them into the trunk of a Cadillac CTS parked at the curb. He climbed into the driver's side as Stanton sat in the passenger seat and secured his seat belt.

"I love the car," Stanton said. "Yours?"

"I wish. This is your car while you're here."

Stanton noticed the slight delay in Scheffield's speech, which was indicative of damage to his Broca's area, the portion of the brain that was just in front of the motor cortex and controlled speech. He wanted to ask about it but knew it would be rude.

Scheffield drove out of the airport and onto the congested freeway. Stanton hadn't been here in a long time, and he was struck by the number of billboards. They were spaced hardly more than fifty feet apart, and the majority advertised personal-injury or criminal-defense lawyers.

"So how long you been with LVPD, Marty?"

"Two years now."

"What'd you do before?"

"I was a student over at UNLV."

"What'd you study?"

"Criminal Justice. I heard you was a professor before being a cop?"

"Yeah, psychology."

"Do you really have a PhD?"

"Yeah."

"So why are you still a cop? If I had a PhD, I wouldn't be a cop."

Stanton grinned. "It's hard to do too much good grading papers."

"Well I'll take that over getting shot at, I'll tell you what."

Stanton began searching restaurants on his phone.

"Where do you think the best pizza is, Marty?"

"Um, pizza? Probably the Pie at Caesar's Palace."

"Can we stop there really quick?"

"Yeah, sure."

The strip was clogged with cars, cabs, trucks carrying billboards for strippers and escorts, and the occasional city bus. Stanton watched the shows playing on the large screens set up near the roadside by the casinos. Then Marty pulled the car to a stop out front of Caesar's Palace.

"I'll be right back," Stanton said.

He took two wrong turns before he asked one of the employees in a clothing store where he could find the Pie. She pointed him toward the fountains. He ordered three pizzas and pasta then waited near the fountains while his order was prepared. The water was far louder than he'd expected it to be, and the people sitting outside the restaurant couldn't hear each other over the noise unless they yelled.

He looked around at the statues which imitated the original marble statues in Italy, remnants of Rome and the Renaissance. They portrayed an ideal of physical and intellectual perfection that he felt had been lost through the centuries. While his culture emphasized the physical, they had demonized the intellectual. He had heard one of his professors say that modern humanity lived as half-men.

The hostess signaled to him that his order was ready. After he paid, he strolled back to the car, and found Marty smoking while sitting on the hood.

"What are the pizzas for?"

"Just a welcoming gift."

Because of the traffic, the trip to the precinct on Martin Luther King Boulevard took nearly an hour. The precinct office building was a modern design, made of steel and glass. Where the Northern Precinct in San Diego was neglected and forgotten, the Las Vegas Metro Police headquarters looked as though it were being constantly cleaned and renovated, as did the surrounding property.

Marty parked up front in a reserved spot. Stanton got out then had to wait for Marty to tuck in his shirt which had come out in the back. The pizzas were cold now and he could feel the grease soaking through the boxes.

They walked into a building that ignored them. Uniforms, detectives, sheriffs, lieutenants, secretaries, lawyers, and paralegals bustled from one room to the next, answering calls and having meetings. The energy was vibrant, and Stanton could feel the drive of the people in the building. They were focused and disciplined. He watched them just a little too long, and Marty asked him if he was okay.

"Fine."

"Sheriff Hall's office is upstairs."

They took an elevator to the top floor, then Marty led him down a long hallway to a corner office.

"I'll see if I can find him."

Stanton sat down in the brown leather chair set out for guests. The office was cluttered but not messy, and it was filled with photographs of Orson with sports figures and politicians. In each one, he was wearing finely tailored suits. Not a single photograph showed him in a uniform.

"Jon Stanton," a voice bellowed. "Didn't think you had the

balls to come back here after the ass-kicking you took from me last time."

Stanton smiled and rose to shake Orson's hand. "Two strings on my racquet were loose and you wouldn't stop long enough for me to grab a new one."

"Your racquet was fine. It was your attitude that was bad. You think too much and choke. You gotta learn to turn off your brain sometimes."

"It may not turn back on, as you've demonstrated."

Orson laughed as he went behind the desk and sat down. "How the hell are you?"

"Good. Better than I've been in a long time. How's everything here? You keeping this cesspool relatively clean?"

"You have no idea, brother. San Diego's got its scumbags, but every piece of shit in the world comes here, at least for a couple of nights. We busted someone from Tuvalu few days back for beating up a hooker. You know that Tuvalu was even a country?"

"No."

"Me neither." He played absent-mindedly with a pen on his desk, rolling it a few inches one way then the other. "Sorry as hell to hear about Melissa. She was a good woman."

"She is. Sometimes it just doesn't work. It's nobody's fault."

"Did you have any idea it was coming?"

"Yeah, some. Just a vague feeling. We knew it was over, but we kept trying to make it work for the kids. I think we went on for about six months like that. Then we just couldn't take the denial anymore."

"Well, you're young and good-looking. What the hell would I do if Wendy ever left me, Lord forbid?"

"Probably just get fatter. What have you been eating, by the way?"

"Hey, don't knock it. I can rough n' tumble with the best of them still at two-sixty. Man needs some fat on him to tell the world he doesn't care that much about what it thinks." He leaned forward on his elbows. "I appreciate you coming out here, Jon. I really do."

"I appreciate the vote of confidence, but I really don't know what you expect me to do. You got some of the best detectives in Robbery-Homicide that I've ever seen. I'm sure I can't do anything they haven't done already."

"Maybe, but I gotta try. We're getting desperate. The file's with the assigned detectives. I'll call over and get them to bring it here."

"No, don't do that. Let me meet them on their turf."

"Gotcha. Their names are Jay Reed and Javier Trujillo. Marty'll take you over to 'em when you're ready. Marty's going to be your guide while you're here. He's a good guy but a little slow, so go easy on him. He's had some brain trauma from a motorcycle accident."

"He's great. Thanks, Orson."

"No, thank you. I'm sure you wanna get started so you can get back to the beach, but let me just say, anything you need, you call me directly. You have my new cell number?"

"No."

"I'll text it to you. And Jon, I ain't kiddin'. You call me if you need anything at all."

"I will." Stanton rose. "Hopefully, I won't be a total waste of your money."

"Well, probably, but if you ain't a gambler you got no business being in this town."

Marty was waiting down the hall, his arms crossed, staring at the floor. When he saw Stanton he straightened up. "How'd it go?"

"Fine," Stanton said. "I need to see Jay and Javier."

"They're downstairs."

Walking side by side, they were quiet for a long time. Then Marty asked, "Did Sheriff Hall say anything about me?"

"He said you're a good cop and that you're going to be showing me around while I'm here."

"Yeah, it should be fun. I've lived here since I was born. I know all the fun places. I thought tonight you'd want to go to a club.

It's a good place to meet people when you don't know anybody."

"I appreciate that, but I'll probably just head back to the hotel after I'm done here."

"Oh, okay."

On the walk back to the elevator, Stanton watched Marty's footsteps. He hadn't noticed it before because he wasn't looking for it, but Marty had a spastic gait: a stiff walk dragging a foot, caused by contractions of the muscles on one side of the leg. It was typically attributed to a conversion disorder, which was a quasi-scientific way of saying that science couldn't explain the cause. Typically, symptoms appeared after stressful events and could be as severe as blindness or complete paralysis. Psychotherapy was the only known cure.

They got down to the first floor and hurried through the maze of corridors before reaching a door marked ROBBERY-HOMI-CIDE. Stanton went to open the door, but Marty grabbed his arm.

"Did Sheriff Hall tell you about Captain Parr?"

"No."

"Well... just be careful, okay?"

"I will. Thanks, Marty."

Marty nodded then walked away, glancing back once before stepping onto the elevator.

6

Stanton waited nearly twenty minutes before the detectives were ready to see him. Instead of sitting at their desks, they were in an interrogation room, where a video was set up. Stanton walked in and waited by the door. The two of them were sitting a couple of feet from a television, watching a boxing match.

"I thought you guys might be hungry," he said, placing the pizzas down on a large table.

The two detectives turned to him. Jay was tall with red hair and wearing a crisp white shirt with suspenders. Javier wore a t-shirt, his badge clipped to his belt. Tattoos ran from his wrists to his elbows.

"You must be Orson's boy," Jay said. "Come in to clean up the mess, huh?"

"Just here to look at some evidence, as a favor."

Javier opened a pizza box and took a slice, folding it in half before taking a large bite.

Stanton sat down.

"I'm Homicide, too, and I could tell you what I would think if my boss brought in some jerk from another city to look at my case. But it's not like that. He offered me a free trip if I would look over the evidence. I couldn't say no to that." Stanton waited a beat before adding, "Besides, IAD's investigating me back home. Seemed like a good time to leave."

Jay watched him. Stanton could see the change in his face, his posture; the way his hands fell. The minutiae that others were blind to screamed at Stanton as loudly as any bold actions. He had noticed those sorts of things since childhood.

"What're they on your ass for?" Jay asked.

"Shooting. Perp held a young girl and her baby hostage. I got off one round that hit him in the throat but caught her shoulder."

Jay shook his head. "Pricks. That's why they're in IA, you know. They can't hack it anywhere else. Any monkey can push papers behind a desk."

Javier added, "They had a file on me last year."

"Oh yeah? For what?"

"Conduct unbecoming."

Jay smirked. "He smacked around some junkie a little and said he was gonna make him eat his entire stash if he didn't testify against his buddy. Someone recorded it on their phone."

"You gotta do what you gotta do sometimes, right?" Javier said, wiping the grease off his lips with the back of his hand. He watched Stanton a second and then sighed. "Hang on."

He left for a second before coming back in with an envelope. It held a DVD. He inserted it into the player underneath the television and said, "This is the video."

A still photo on the television showed an empty portion of what looked like a subway train or bus. The camera was positioned on the ceiling, capturing about ten square feet of space.

"This is the tram up there on the Strip."

The video began to play. There was no sound, but the images were clear. It was the car at the end of the tram. A few people piled on and the tram raced across the Las Vegas Strip, twenty feet above the ground. Three people got off at one of the stops, and a female and male couple came into view. They were middle-aged, perhaps in their fifties. The male had a fake tan and wore a tuxedo. The female was blonde with her hair pulled up, wearing a red jacket over a black evening gown. They were kissing and joking. From their mannerisms, Stanton could tell they were thoroughly drunk.

Then, just as the tram started moving, the woman's face contorted with fear and she screamed. The man jumped to his feet then held up his hands as if he were surrendering. Another person came into view from the bottom of the screen. He was wearing a green jacket and had a ski mask over his head. He pointed a handgun at the man's head.

The man in the ski mask grabbed the woman by her hair, nearly lifting her off her feet. He threw her against one of the seats while keeping the gun aimed steadily at the man's head. He bent her over, lifted her dress, pulled down his pants, and raped her.

The man in the tuxedo watched and shouted something but didn't intervene. Stanton kept his eyes on the screen. The video pained him, but he could shut down that part of himself. The part that screamed to him how horrific the scene was. When he shut that off, he could function. He could watch the video and keep going.

Finally, the man in the tux lunged at the rapist, who shot him twice in the head. The rapist then pressed the gun to the back of the woman's head and pulled the trigger just as the tram came to a stop. He then moved out of view.

Javier turned the video off. "The *cojones* on this guy. That was the Flamingo and Caesar's Palace stop, right in the middle of the line. He could've been seen by a hundred people, and he didn't give a shit."

"How many witnesses?"

"Not one," Jay said. "Haven't found a single witness. He picked the perfect time and place."

"Did you go to the media?"

"Posted some of the video and they played it on all four major stations. Nothing."

Stanton ran his tongue along his teeth, a habit he had when lost in thought. "Who were they?"

Javier got another slice of pizza. "Daniel and Emily Steed. Residents of Vegas."

"Any reason why a guy in a tuxedo is riding the tram?"

Jay shrugged. "People get wasted all the time and take the

tram home to avoid driving."

Jay had misunderstood the question. A man who could afford a tuxedo like that could easily hire a limousine or a cab. He didn't need to ride the tram with the public.

"Do you need to watch it again?" Javier asked.

"Not right now. Would you guys mind if I got a copy of the file to take to my hotel room?"

The two detectives looked at each other. Then Javier said, "I guess that's okay."

"I'll get everything back to you as soon as I'm done." Stanton rose. "It was nice meeting you guys."

Javier nodded, but Jay turned back to the video without saying a word. As Stanton walked out, he knew instinctively that the file would be missing the most important details. His finding the killer would be the worst-case scenario for those two. They'd be humiliated that an outsider had to be brought in because they couldn't get the job done.

Stanton knew they would do everything in their power to slow him down from finding the man on that video.

7

Stanton found Marty near the entrance of police headquarters, sipping a Coke and reading a magazine about car repair.

"Are you done?" Marty asked.

"Yeah. Mind giving me a lift back to the hotel?"

"The car is yours." He pulled out the keys and handed them to Stanton. "It's a rental."

"Thanks. Marty, I need the file on the Steed murders. Any way you could get that to me without having to go through Jay and Javier?"

"No way. Parr would have my ass. They're the assigned detectives, so no one looks at the file without their permission."

"I could get it for you," a voice behind him said.

Stanton turned to see a young woman in a police uniform, with straight red hair that came down to her shoulders.

"Hi," she said, holding out her hand. "I'm Mindi Morgan. I'm the assistant assigned to you."

"I thought Marty was."

"He is. I guess I meant I'm also your assistant. Sheriff Hall thought you might need both of us since Marty isn't in top form nowadays."

Marty looked at the ground and was quiet a moment before saying, "I'm a little slow, Jon. I forget things sometimes."

"I don't find you slow at all." He turned to Mindi. "Tell the Sheriff I'm fine with Marty."

Marty perked up, a grin on his face. Stanton thanked Mindi again for her offer, then left the building with Marty.

"Marty, I need that file. I know Jay and Javier are your friends, but—"

"They're not my friends. My mom used to say you don't know what people really think of you until you hear them behind your back. I heard them once. They're not my friends. I'll see if I can get you that file."

"Thanks. I'm over at the Mirage." He took out one of his cards and wrote his cell number on it. "Call me when you find anything out."

Stanton got into the car.

"Jon, thanks," Marty blurted out.

"It's okay, Marty. Just get me that file."

Stanton used the valet at the Mirage. Since he'd been there last, the casino had set up a new street display for the throngs of tourists going past. It was something about volcanoes. Surrounded by lush vegetation, it appeared like an oasis among the crowded streets of the Vegas Strip.

He walked through the lobby and over a small bridge connecting the hotel to the casino. The smell of liquor and smoke was strong, and there were no windows or clocks. This was to trick the gamblers so they wouldn't know the time and would gamble freely without worrying about anything outside the casino.

During his time as a graduate student of psychology, Stanton had researched the tactics used by casinos to optimize gambling for a class on limbic system manipulation in marketing. The goal of the casino was to literally recreate the womb, a place of comfort on a primitive level. The colors of the rooms were primarily red or soft orange, and mild music was always on a continuous loop to maintain the constant rhythm. During the '80s and '90s, casinos released pheromones through the air conditioning systems to encourage aggressive gambling. When a group of Brigham Young University sociology students discovered the tactic, the casinos stopped it immediately and denied ever doing it.

Stanton found the elevator and headed to the nineteenth floor. His room was halfway down the hall. The curtains were open, revealing a view of the Strip. He kicked off his shoes, turned off his cell phone, and collapsed onto the bed. He was asleep before he could even think about the video that he'd been running through his mind all the way there.

When Stanton woke it was to the sound of airplanes flying overhead. He looked at the clock: 3:36 pm. He went to the window. He was surprised how many families were down on the street, pushing strollers and hauling shopping bags. As the economy soured and fewer people came to gamble, the tourism board was attempting to remake the city into a family-friendly destination by focusing on the shows and the shopping.

Stanton soaked in the tub for an hour before getting out and dressing. As he was putting on his shirt, there was a knock at his door. He finished buttoning and answered. Mindi stood there, a thick file in hand.

"Can I come in?"

"Sure."

She entered and looked around. "Nice pad. This is one of the nicer hotels here."

"I've always liked it."

She turned to him. "I have the file you want."

She put it down on a table and sat down on a sofa near the windows.

"I asked Marty to get it for me."

"Have I done something to offend you or something?"

"I didn't appreciate how you treated Marty."

"It was the truth."

"It was humiliating." Stanton sat on the edge of the bed. "What happened to him?"

"He used to ride a motorcycle everywhere, a nice Harley he'd saved for, like, five years to get. When his wife left him, you couldn't get him off that thing. 'Bout six years ago he was out on the freeway and his bike flipped over. He landed square on his head. His helmet saved his life, but it... well, you've seen him. It was totally random. They think the front tire hit a rock or something but they're not sure. Sometimes, life just takes you where it wants to I guess."

"He doesn't deserve to be treated like that."

She sighed. "Fine, I promise you, I will not speak to him that way again."

"That was quick. Out of curiosity, why do you care what I say? I'm not your boss."

"Because this is the biggest story in the state right now, and I think you can catch who did it."

"And you want to be there when I do. Is that it?"

"Girl's gotta have ambitions. Do you know how hard it is for a female to rise in a police department? Any police department, much less the locker room of Vegas Metro? I need any advantage I can get. When I heard Orson was bringing you in, I asked to be assigned to you."

"Why? I can't do anything differently than Jay or Javier."

"That's bullshit and we both know it. I looked you up. I'd actually looked you up before this case. Orson talks about you more than you know. He thinks you're psychic."

"Well, I'm not."

"It doesn't matter. What matters is that he thinks you are, and he's throwing everything he has at you to solve this." She pointed to the file. "That guy was one of the richest men in Nevada. His allies in the legislature, the mayor, and even the governor have called us, asking about the case. They've lost out on a big donor and the estate's been handed over to his son, who's not doling out anything until the murderer's caught. Like it or not, this is gonna be as high-profile as it gets."

"I've never cared about that. That's not why I'm here. And I don't need your help."

"Yes you do. You just don't know it." She stood up. "I have connections that Marty doesn't have—that even Orson doesn't have. You're gonna need 'em. Let me know when you're ready." As she walked out, she glanced to him and said, "Sorry to hear about your divorce."

After she was gone, Stanton turned to the file on the table. Inside was the sum total of two lives that had been extinguished in mere minutes. Stanton would have to comprehend that madness in a way that made him sick; he would recreate what the killer had done and feel what he'd felt. When working cases, he had insomnia at best and outright manifestations of physical ailments at worst. He had thrown up blood, been constipated, ran fevers of over one hundred degrees... each case took a piece of him that he never got back.

He was going to know this madness, but first he would have to know Daniel and Emily Steed.

8

Stanton lifted the Steed file and felt its weight. The hotel was quiet at this time of day, and all he could hear was the shower running in another room. He tucked the file under his arm and headed out the door to the casino.

He stood at the edge of the slot machines for a while, watching the faces of the gamblers. Some were young but most were old. They were playing a losing game that was rigged against them from the beginning, yet they still maintained hope that somehow, some way, they would win against fate. A person might be able to defeat chance, Stanton thought, but no one could defeat fate.

He went to a Japanese restaurant up on a platform, a sleek design of black and red, and sat at one of the booths over the casino floor. He ordered an orange juice and a J roll of sushi then opened the file. The first few pages contained a brief bio issued by the company Daniel Steed had founded.

Daniel Steed came from a generation that Stanton hadn't been sure existed anymore. He was born in Jackson, Wyoming, to David and Bethany Steed. David was a miner, and Bethany was a homemaker for Daniel and his five siblings. He'd earned average grades in school, but when he was twelve, he went to work in the mines. He saved every penny he made for five years, and when he was seventeen years old, he struck out for California. He got as far as Las Vegas before the Vietnam War broke out.

The file said that Daniel had served two tours in Vietnam, and that was the only mention of his time in the war. Stanton had seen similar silences on many occasions. Most Vietnam veterans refused to speak about their experiences.

At twenty-three, Daniel bought his own company, a small motel with a few slot machines. He had borrowed heavily to turn the motel around. Within ten years, he owned two casinos, several restaurants, and a private golf course. By the age of forty-five, his real estate holdings and casinos had made him a billionaire, and he had officially retired.

His wife, Emily, was the typical spouse of a man like Daniel. She came from an affluent family and had been a model, appearing briefly in Levi's commercials in the '80s. At thirty-two she met Daniel and they married six months later. They had one son, Fredrick Steed, who purportedly lived in Las Vegas although the file didn't provide an address.

The rest of the file consisted of financial records, credit reports, court records, birth certificates, copies of social security cards, death certificates, police narratives, CAD call logs from dispatch, and clippings of media reports, as well as lists of the Steeds' neighbors, business associates, and relatives. The autopsy reports were extraordinarily detailed, far more than they needed to be—a sign of the couple's influence.

There were two ballistics reports, one from the Las Vegas Crime Lab and one from a private expert hired out of Portland. Both had come to the same conclusion: The man in the ski mask had used a 9mm. The private expert had identified the make of the gun as a Smith & Wesson, where the crime lab in Vegas thought it was a Beretta. The rifling impressions, the scratches found on the bullet that had been fired, were chaotic, and in some places even vertical. They had been purposely altered with a metallic wire shoved into the barrel of the gun so ballistics couldn't accurately identify the weapon used. On the street it was called a "rat's tail." Few people knew about rat's tails. Those who did usually learned about them while serving time in prison.

Mindi had even included handwritten notes taken by Jay and Javier during the investigation. Files never included the internal handwritten notes written by the investigators, and even the prosecutors and defense attorneys never saw those. She was good.

Stanton read the police narratives, but they were little more than descriptions of what he'd already seen on the video. They did include one interesting note about Bill James, a business partner of Daniel's who had sued him over a real estate deal. He had been interviewed, and his alibi—he'd been in Los Angeles at the time—had checked out.

At face value, the detectives were saying that the case was open and under investigation for possible suspects. Reading between the lines, however, Stanton knew they had made up their minds that this was a random attack akin to a shark attack. It didn't happen often, but when it did it was devastating.

That very well could have been what it was, but something told him it wasn't. At the end of the file, attached in a paper slip, was a copy of the video. Stanton went to the hotel lobby where he asked the front desk about computers that were for guest use. The concierge arranged for a laptop to be delivered to Stanton's room.

When the computer arrived, Stanton tipped the bellboy then put the disc into the laptop. He immediately recognized the end cabin of the tram. He watched the video, then watched it again. He put it on a slow forward, going through it frame by frame.

Emily was facing forward when she screamed. There were doors on her right and left but she didn't look at either, which meant the unsub—unknown subject—had been on the tram already. They would have noticed someone in a ski mask, so he must not have had it on beforehand. The only person who could have done such a thing without worrying about being seen would be someone who had planned to kill the witnesses.

Stanton watched the sexual assault. He watched it again and again, until he no longer felt the tug of emotion in his gut telling him to pity this woman.

For the unsub to grab Mrs. Steed and bend her over only took a few seconds. He penetrated her from behind shortly after, taking perhaps no more than three seconds. How could he have gotten an erection in three seconds?

He may have already had an erection. Studies performed on sex offenders had shown that violence, as much as sex, aroused a certain population. Penial studies measuring the arousal time during different video and audio stimuli showed that in over thirty percent of incarcerated sex offenders, scenes of violence caused an erection as quickly as pornography did.

Stanton took out the disc and placed it back in the file before closing the laptop. The images were in his head now; they were part of him, along with the thousands of others he had absorbed in his time as a Homicide and Sex Crimes detective. He needed to depressurize, to spend a significant amount of time doing something other than working the case. Once his head was clear, he could work the case without having to watch the video again.

He picked up the phone and called Marty.

"Hey," he said. "I'd like to see some of these fun spots you were telling me about."

9

Bill James woke with a start. His eyes darted open to see himself looking back at him. He realized he was lying on his back in his bed, looking up at his mirrored ceiling. The two women next to him wore nothing but high heels and he watched them for a while, running his eyes over the perfect curves of their bodies. He had seen a thousand girls like them. They came to the city looking for success, only to learn that the way to achieve success in Vegas was to sell everything—not just their bodies, but also their souls. Soon they would be burnt-out junkies like the thousands who were already plastered over the city. For sale to any degenerate who had sixty bucks.

He rolled out of bed and into his slippers. James glanced out the windows at the city below. His suite was made up of all windows with only one solid wall, a design specification he had requested. He wanted as much sunlight as he could get during the day and as much neon light as he could get at night. He guessed from the dimming daylight that it was probably around five or six o'clock.

He used the bathroom, showered, and pulled out a Polo suit with purple pinstripes from his enormous closet before heading down to the casino floor. When he was depressed or anxious, he went there to watch the action. He hadn't gambled in over thirty years, and he didn't see the draw of it, but he knew it didn't need a draw. He watched people's eyes. They were almost in a trance.

"Morning, Boss."

He turned to see his floor manager, Timmy Rodriguez, come up beside him.

"Heard you had a scuffle," James said.

"Nothing we couldn't handle. Just some drunk who got pissed off. We got a bigger problem, though."

"What?"

"High rollers' room. Guy there's playing blackjack hard and fast, eighty or ninety grand a hand. House is down over a million."

"Who is he?"

"Never seen him before. He wasn't in Vanessa."

James pulled a thin cigar from a gold case he kept in the inside pocket of his jacket and lit it as he headed to the human resources office. Vanessa was the computer database they used to keep track of the proficient gamblers, usually just the whales—the high rollers—who came, gambled big and fast, and left with his money. There was only one way to beat the casinos: quit while you were ahead. The longer gamblers played, the longer the casino's edge wore them down. If this man's profile wasn't found in Vanessa, then he was either getting lucky or he was a new whale on the scene.

The high roller room was elegantly designed. James had brought the designer from Paris after he had designed the Prime Minister's vacation home. The designer was a jerk, and James had nearly thrown him out on his ass, but his work was so good that James tolerated him until the project was complete.

The room had a type of soft lighting that was rarely found outside of the best five-star restaurants in the world. The rugs had been imported illegally from Iran because of an embargo. The tables were handmade with the finest wood available. The glasses were crystal with a hint of sapphire that glinted blue in the right light. The felt on the tables was handmade specifically for this room. He'd spared no expense.

Three tables were in play—two on the far right and one on the left. A crowd surrounded the one on the left, and a portly man in an excellent gray suit was seated in the middle. James came up behind him and softly brushed aside some of the spectators. Timmy hadn't been exaggerating. The man was currently betting over one hundred thousand dollars on this hand. He was betting big and fast, hitting a hot streak, and he probably knew when to quit. He was up by almost two million dollars—two million dollars of James's money.

James went around the table and looked into the man's eyes. He could find what he was looking for there. The face could smile, the hands could rise in triumph, the voice could cheer, but the eyes couldn't betray what someone actually felt. And his eyes told James, "I don't care."

That was a hallmark of a degenerate gambler: the thrill of winning didn't matter anymore. They gambled to gamble. Winning wasn't the goal. They were the gamblers who lost homes, retirement accounts, college funds, cars and grocery money.

James relieved his dealer and took his place. "That's quite a hot streak you're on," he said.

"When it hits, it hits."

"Bill James." He held out his hand.

The man shook. "Greg Fontenot."

James expertly shuffled the cards and dealt the hand. "Where you from, Greg?"

"Dallas."

"Really? I own some property in Dallas. Try to get up there every so often."

Greg stayed at eighteen. James hit at fifteen and got the ten of hearts. The crowd cheered and clapped. A woman wrapped her hands around Greg's shoulders and kissed him on the cheek.

"Greg, you don't enjoy this game. I can tell. For real gamblers like us, this isn't it. How 'bout we show these folks what gambling really is?"

"How's that?"

"Those chips you got there, I'll match 'em. One hand. Winner takes all."

"Don't do it, baby," the woman said. "Let's take what we got and go."

The woman was clearly his wife, but in that moment James understood him better than she did.

"Let's do it! Let it ride!"

The crowd cheered as his wife tried to talk him out of it, but she was too late. His eyes were wide and stared at the table as though he wanted to make love to it. In fact, James wouldn't have been surprised if Greg were sexually aroused. He'd seen it before.

James turned to Timmy. "How much does he have in chips?"

Timmy counted. "One million, eight hundred, and twenty-six thousand."

"Get me a marker for that amount."

Timmy wrote something on his phone, and another dealer ran in thirty seconds later with a slip, which he handed to James.

James put the slip on the table. "You ready?"

Greg looked as though he might faint. He was filled with lust, excitement and avarice. His wife was yelling at him, physically attempting to pull him away from the tables. He pushed her away aggressively.

James smiled and dealt the cards. Greg glanced at his hand but had no reaction. James peeked at his cards. Greg brushed toward himself on the table, indicating he wanted another card. James dealt it: the six of clubs. That brought his hand to twenty.

"I'll stay."

His wife gasped, her fingers turning white from squeezing his shoulder. James could tell that even a tractor couldn't have pulled her away from the table right then.

James flipped his cards, revealing the three of hearts and the Jack of spades. He pulled out the next card slowly, enjoying the look of panic and ecstasy on Greg's face. It was the eight of hearts.

Greg folded as if the air had been knocked out of him. His wife slapped his face and stormed away.

"Nice playing with you," James said as the dealer began collecting the chips.

James walked away, and Timmy followed. He walked across the casino floor, excitement in his belly.

"The gambling commission's not going to like that," Timmy said.

"Call Mike Connors over there. Tell him to take care of it."

Timmy made note of it in his phone then said, "That would've been a big hit. Four million dollars."

"Most gamblers get their training from other gamblers. You know where they should start?"

"Where?"

James stepped into the corner near the men's room where he knew the eye in the sky wasn't monitoring. "A magician." He pulled out a ten of clubs, a two of diamonds, a five of diamonds and several other cards from his sleeve. "Get rid of these."

Timmy smirked. "Yes, sir."

James took a quick piss then washed his hands. He had actually enjoyed that hand, but it still felt empty to him. Regardless, no one was going anywhere with four million dollars of his money.

As James was stepping out of the bathroom, Milton Henry approached him.

"There you are. Where you been?"

"Didn't know my CEO got to ask me that and treat me like some asshole."

"I didn't... I wasn't saying—"

"I'm just kidding, Milt. You need to relax. What do you need?"

"Cal Robertson's here and he's causing a scene. They called me down to take care of it, but he threw a drink in my face and called me a kike."

"Where is he?"

"Near the stage."

James walked briskly through the casino and across the bridge over the strip. The casino occupied two buildings; he and Raj had come up with the idea together. One contained all the shops, shows, and attractions. The other was solely for gambling, a place where the hardcore gamblers could be alone while their families whittled away their time watching dance numbers and magic shows.

He made his way past the act on stage and saw that several of his guards had cornered Cal. He was ranting, flailing his arms and shouting so loud that people were turning to look at him. James brushed past his men and grabbed Cal's arm.

"What the fuck are you doing? Are you drunk again?"

"You son of a bitch," Cal said, ripping his arm away. "You son of a bitch! I'll have your ass, you cocksucker. She was nineteen."

"I don't know what you're talking about."

"Fuck you!"

He spit in James's face. Milton handed him a handkerchief and he calmly wiped the spit off.

"You need to calm down, Calvin. I don't know what you're talking about."

"I'm meeting with the board. You're a psychopath, you cocksucker. We're throwing your ass back to the ghetto you came from. And maybe I'll have a talk with the cops, huh? I know what you did to Daniel, too."

"I had nothing to do with that."

"Bullshit. You always hated his guts. You're a murderer on top of a fucking cocksucker."

"Get out of my casino." James glanced around quickly and saw that only a handful of people were watching.

"It's not your casino, you—"

Before Cal could finish his sentence, James bashed his fist into his jaw, knocking him back. One of his men grabbed Cal, and before he could open his mouth, James had struck him in the chest and smashed a haymaker into the other side of his jaw.

"Get him outta here."

James watched as his men dragged away a barely conscious Cal Robertson. He put his hands on his hips and swore under his breath.

"That's not good, Boss."

"You don't need to tell me. Um, get... um, shit. First, get me some fucking ice for my hand, then get the board on the line."

"Everyone?"

"Everyone."

10

Leaning against the Cadillac, Stanton waited for Marty out on the curb. He was reading on his phone when a valet came up to him.

"Nice car."

"Thanks. It's not mine. Just a rental."

"Still, all a man needs is to drive that around for a little bit."

"You think so?"

He shrugged. "I don't know. You seem happy enough." He glanced back to make sure no one waited on him. "Whatcha readin'?"

"Ecclesiastes."

"Never heard of it."

"It's in the Old Testament. It's my favorite book from the Bible."

"Oh, you a Christian man? Well that's cool. We see a lotta your folk down here. I'm Baptist myself. You?"

"Mormon."

"No shit? Let me tell you, man, I went down to Park City for that Sundance Film Festival. Ain't never been treated better by folks in my life. You Mormons is okay with me."

"See any good movies down there?"

"Nah, I go for the food and the sight-seein'. Them movies is all messed up. Made by the celebrities I see up in here every day, and them folks is *really* messed up. Like someone said, 'They walk around like they so fine, but their assholes smell just like mine.' You know what I'm sayin'?"

He grinned. "Yeah, I do."

Marty pulled up in a police cruiser. He rolled down his window and shouted, "Should we take your car?"

"Yeah." Stanton turned to the valet. "Is he okay to park out here?"

"Yeah, just leave it over there. I'll keep an eye on it."

Stanton handed him a twenty-dollar bill. "Thanks."

Marty parked then hopped into the passenger seat of the Cadillac as Stanton adjusted the mirrors and put on his seat belt. He pulled out of the Mirage's lot and onto the strip. It was beginning to get crowded.

"Where we going, Marty?"

"We can get dinner and watch a comedy show at the Havana. It's a hotel just up the street by the Luxor."

They drove past massive screens displaying women in G-strings and leotards dancing on a stage, videos of comedians making crowds roar with laughter, and magicians making explosions on stage while lions and women ran around behind them.

"There it is."

The casino was large and connected to another building by a bridge that went over the street. It lit up the evening sky and had lights that shot straight up from the top of the two buildings, seemingly into space.

"Crazy, huh?"

"Never seen anything like it."

They pulled up to the valet and got out. The valets, who were dressed all in black, addressed everyone as "sir" or "madam." Stanton followed Marty through the large doors with gold leaf trim into the building.

Inside, it looked like a carnival. In fact rides were set up for the children, and arrows pointed to hallways that led to magicians, comedians, dance shows and restaurants. Most of the people were with their families.

"Is this the casino?" Stanton asked.

"No, that's the second building. They keep everything separate here."

He followed Marty up a hallway past a stage. Several men in suits and a couple of uniformed officers were standing by. An older gentleman was shouting and swearing while a younger man tried to calm him down. Stanton couldn't hear what was said, but he saw the older man throw a drink into the younger man's face. The younger man wiped it off with a napkin and walked away.

They headed up the hallway to the comedy theater and took their seats near the front. A black-and-white checkerboard served as a curtain, and a spotlight shone down on the microphone.

Marty motioned to a vendor who was standing near their seats and ordered a couple popcorns and Cokes. The popcorn came drizzled with butter. Stanton took a few bites and could taste sugar on it as well.

"I know Mindi brought the file to you," Marty said, his eyes focused on his popcorn.

"I didn't ask her to."

"It's okay. She can do things I can't do. If we can find the person who did this, it will be better."

"Marty, I want you to listen to me. You are no different than anybody else, okay? Don't ever let anyone tell you that you are. We all have our strong points and our weak points. That's what makes us human."

"I can remember what I was like before. I was really smart. Now it's hard to think. My words are good, but I can't concentrate and I forget everything."

"You're doing just fine."

He didn't speak for a while. "I was married once, you know."

"What happened?"

"She left me. She said she didn't want to take care of me and that I wasn't making her happy. I don't blame her."

"I was married, too. She left me as well." He held up his coke in a toast. "To not finding another wife who'll leave us."

Marty smiled. He turned back to his popcorn with zeal and

seemed to be in a better mood.

"I gotta use the bathroom," Stanton said. "I'll be right back."

He walked outside and down the hallway toward the rest-room, where he heard someone shouting again. He walked out to the main lobby and saw the same older man yelling at an-other man, different than the one Stanton had seen him shout-ing at before. The man being shouted at was dressed impec-cably. Slicked back hair and a thick, dark, mustache.

Suddenly, the new man looked around, then belted the shout-ing man in the face. Two more blows and the shouting man was nearly unconscious.

Stanton watched as he was dragged from the building, and no one even seemed to notice.

11

Stanton dressed and showered before seven in the morning then ate a quick meal of eggs and fruit at the buffet in his hotel. He watched the families and the couples who were there, but he was mostly interested in the individuals who sat quietly at their tables with bloodshot eyes, barely eating their meals. He knew their minds were still in the casinos.

When he finished his meal, he got his car from the valet and drove to the Metro PD headquarters. Mindi was waiting for him outside in jeans and a leather jacket.

"Mind if I hitch a ride?" she asked.

"Where's Marty?"

"He had some work to catch up on."

"I thought he was only assigned to me?"

"Look, I know you want to go see the Steeds' house. Marty can't get you in there." She pulled out a key and held it up. "But I can. Do you want to go or not?"

"Fine. Get in. But tell me where Marty is."

"I wasn't lying. He had a bunch of paperwork from old tickets and he had to catch up on it. I told him I would cover this."

Stanton typed the address into his phone's GPS and pulled away from the curb. He rolled down the window to get some fresh air, but the air outside was worse. Exhaust fumes and the pungent odors of sweaty crowds and burning neon tainted the air.

"You know, you really should be nicer to me. I can help you a lot."

"I saw you got Jay and Javier's notes in the file. How'd you do that?"

"Do you really wanna know or are you just asking to make small talk? Because if it's small talk, it's probably best you not ask."

They drove in silence for a few minutes before Mindi said, "Your partner almost killed you once. I read that about you. Eli Sherman, right?"

"Yeah."

"My partner, my first real partner, was a guy named Lawrence Zira. He was from Bosnia. He… he was married, but we had an affair. Well, he had an affair. I was twenty-one and an idiot. He didn't tell me he was married. No one in the precinct told me— not my bosses, not the other uniforms. No one. I was in the dark until a receptionist finally pulled me aside and told me about it. When I confronted him, he laughed at me."

Stanton glanced at her. "I'm sorry."

"Don't be, it taught me a good lesson. He was a dirtbag, but I've never forgotten that no one told me."

Stanton turned right at an intersection, where a man was dancing and shouting at the passersby.

"He killed twelve girls that we know of," he said. "That's the only reason he joined the police force. He liked the opportunity to find victims."

"Don't they screen for people like him?"

"They do, but some psychopaths, the ones who are high-functioning, can't be detected. Most psychopaths are self-destructive. In my clinical internship, we had a patient who was considered a pure psychopath. She would try to break open her skull every day to pick at her brain. She had to be restrained most of the time. That's a true psychopath. The manipulative sadist is a much rarer kind of psychopath, and we don't understand them. You could live your whole life next to one and never know what they really are inside. You only see what they want you to see."

"Or maybe what *you* want to see."

"Yeah, maybe."

He sped up a winding road to the affluent suburb of Cottonwood Hills and came to a stop at a large three-story home. It looked much like a well-manicured log cabin, with the exception of the yellowing lawn and the untrimmed bushes and flowers.

"I'd like to go in by myself."

She handed him the key without objection. "I'll be here."

Stanton grabbed the Steed file from the backseat.

He walked up the driveway and stood on the porch, staring at the front door before inserting the key. He opened the door then stepped inside and closed it behind him. All the blinds had been shut and the place smelled like dust.

From where he stood he could see into the kitchen, which was directly in front of him. The living room was to his right, along with several bedrooms and a den. He walked over to a sofa and sat down. It didn't appear like the home of a billionaire. Stanton wondered if Steed had been excessively frugal.

A massive projector hung from the ceiling, and the handcrafted furniture was chocolate-colored wood. A large portrait of Daniel Steed standing behind his wife, who was seated in front of him, took up half a wall. A few photos of them with friends and family sat on a side table. He didn't see anyone who resembled Emily or Daniel enough to be their son. He scanned the photos then opened his file and found the photograph of Fredrick Steed. The young man wasn't in any of the family photos. Stanton made a note of that in the file.

Stanton rose and walked around the house. He peeked into the bedrooms, the kitchen, and the main bathroom. Mrs. Steed's robe was hanging over the shower rod. Rather than giving the room a homey feel, it made it feel empty.

He walked back to the living room. He skimmed the discs in the entertainment center DVD rack. Two had blank spaces where the titles should've been, and he took them out of their cases. One was labeled *Family Reunion, 1998*. The other had no label. He found the remotes to the projector and the DVD player and fiddled with them until they turned on. He inserted the family reunion disc.

As it turned on, Stanton saw a bird's-eye view of the massive casino showroom that had been rented to host the Steed reunion. Then the camera shifted, shut off, and turned back on. It was now held low, about chest height, and he knew a child was filming. He was going around to the different guests, asking them questions and grilling them about what they were wearing. He asked one guest in a hideous blue dress what it felt like to have the ugliest dress at the reunion. Tears welled up in the woman's eyes, and she turned away from the camera and ignored the child. The boy smelled the blood in the water and continued antagonizing her until her husband threatened him. Then he ran off, laughing.

Next the boy harassed a young waitress. When she began to get upset, he said that his father had paid for the reunion, and she had better not piss him off, or he would tattle on her. The waitress, clearly fearing for her job, took the boy's abuse, which consisted of teasing her about her appearance. Stanton was about to fast-forward when the questions the child was asking turned sexual.

The waitress appeared shocked and turned back to someone who looked like her boss standing a few feet away. He noticed her discomfort, came over, and asked what was going on.

"I just asked if she would show me her pussy," the boy said.

The boss, shocked, looked out over the crowd. The boy continued to film and giggle. He turned back to the girl, asking more questions about her genitals. Then, suddenly, the camera shook, and Daniel Steed's face appeared on the screen.

"What did you say to her, you little shit? Huh? What did you say?"

Mrs. Steed's voice was in the background. "Danny, take care of this later. Not here."

"Get the hell outta here before I paint your backside red."

The boy pulled away but left the camera on. Before he got

more than a few feet away, Daniel Steed said, "His father was as big an asshole as he is."

Stanton rewound the disc and played that part again. He guessed that Daniel wasn't talking about himself. He flipped through the police reports. No mention that Fredrick was Emily's son from another marriage.

Stanton watched the rest of the disc, but it consisted of Fredrick playing outside the reunion and sneaking back in to steal drinks from the bar. When the video ended, Stanton made a few notes in the file and put the unlabeled disc into the DVD player.

The disc was blank. He fast-forwarded through it a bit then stopped it. Wondering why they would keep a blank disc with the others, he took it out and slipped it into the file. He scanned the living room again before leaving.

Mindi was on her phone and looked up when he got in the car. He pulled out of the driveway without a word.

"So?" she said.

"We need to pay Fredrick a visit."

12

Sitting on the hood of his Mustang in the middle of a rundown apartment complex, Captain Alma Parr lifted his Browning .45 caliber handgun. The gun was the 1911 model. Browning had designed it for the army, and it had passed the Ordnance Department's highest level of testing for reliability, including the continuous firing of six thousand rounds without jamming. It was the most reliable handgun ever made. The army had dumped it because NATO refused to approve its use. Parr had bought as many as he could find and required his detectives to carry them.

He looked at the fresh tattoo still healing on his right bicep. A dragon ran across his collar bone, over his shoulder, around his bicep and down his forearm to the wrist. He flexed the bulging muscles beneath it a few times and waves spread through the ink, stretching and contracting it.

Parr glanced around him. This was the barrio, L Street-9 territory. They were one of the most dangerous gangs in the state. None of them would think twice to pop a high-ranking cop in broad daylight.

The red-brick complex made a U shape around the courtyard where he was parked right in the middle. He had no backup, no officers undercover. No one even knew he was there.

The tingling of fear in his belly excited him. It made him want it more, to fight harder. Fear was his old buddy, and he looked forward to reuniting with it. It reminded him of his time in the burned-out buildings of Fallujah, left alone with his rifle and only enough rations for one week. *Take out as many shitheads as possible.* Those were the only orders he could remember.

He heard voices nearby. Three men came out of one of the buildings and headed toward an El Camino parked at the curb. They were laughing and one of them threw his head back. Parr could see the outline of a handgun in the front of his pants, tucked in tightly against the belt.

Parr slid off his hood and ducked behind his car. The El Camino was about thirty feet away. He waited until they were closer... just enough. When the men were ten feet from their car, Parr bolted out, his sidearm drawn. He was there so quickly the men stood frozen. Then the one with the handgun went for it, and Parr fired.

The round went clean through the man's hand and he screamed and doubled over, pressing on the wound and trying to stop the flow of blood.

"What the fuck?" yelled another one.

Parr ran up, grabbed him by his throat, and spun around, slamming him against the hood of the El Camino. He reached back and grabbed the handgun out of the other man's pants. The one he'd shot ran off behind an apartment building.

"Get on the ground," Parr said. He complied, and Parr turned his attention to the man he had pinned on the hood. "You lied to me, Mateo."

"About what?"

"You told me Rico was gonna be at the drop with two keys he took off that barbequed body."

"What body, man? I don't know what you talkin' about, white boy."

Parr struck him in the genitals with a knee.

"Shit! *Besa mi culo, puto!*"

Parr grabbed Mateo's genitals, and twisted. Mateo screamed.

"You remember now?"

"All right, man. All right!"

Parr let go. "The body in the car. That's all I care about. I don't give a shit about the keys. You can keep those. I want the concha who merced the body."

"Somebody told Rico 'bout it."

"Somebody or you?"

"No, man, it wasn't me. I swear it, man. On my moms, I swear it."

"Who then?"

"I heard it was a cop."

Parr grabbed Mateo's genitals again and yanked violently, making him scream.

"Don't lie to me, Mateo."

"I ain't lyin'. I swear, man. I ain't lyin'."

He released his grip. "What cop?"

"I don't know, man. I don't know."

"Well you better gimme somethin' if you wanna have kids, *ese.*"

"I heard from my boy, Hector. He said some cop took five G's to tell Rico you all was waitin' for him at the drop."

"What cop? What does he look like?"

"I don't know, man. On my moms, I don't know."

"Give me Hector's address."

"All right, man. I'll give it, I swear."

Parr pulled out his phone and opened a notepad app. "Type."

Mateo typed in an address and handed the phone back. "Yo, you gotta call an ambulance. I think you popped my nuts."

Parr glanced at the address and then back to Mateo. "So? Walk it off."

The address was in a nearby low-income housing project, and Parr knew the area. The homes had been government-subsidized during the real estate boom, and after the crash owners couldn't give them away because no one thought they were even worth the taxes. A few of the wealthier residents had bought them and rented them out to illegal immigrants and vagabonds, people who didn't have identification, credit, or steady employment.

The one thing that always struck Parr about those neighborhoods was the corners. Sometimes as many as twenty young men were wasting their days away there. Street corners were the ghetto forums where gossip was traded along with goods— mostly guns and drugs, but sometimes hookers, illegal porn and false IDs. As he passed a light, a man on a corner held out his arms, challenging him. He chuckled to himself and continued driving.

The red-brick home at the address Mateo had given him was a modest two-story with a lawn that looked as if it hadn't been cut in years. He drove past it then spun around the block before parking two houses away. Parr leaned back in his seat and watched.

The neighborhood was quiet and no one waited on the corners. Even the pit bulls, which he knew should be prominently displayed, were inside. The locals had been tipped off.

He punched his steering wheel. "Damn it!" He would have to pay another visit to Mateo.

As he reached down to turn on the car, he saw the curtains of the home he was watching open about six inches then close quickly. Mateo could deny he'd tipped off Hector, but he couldn't deny it if he had given Parr the wrong address. Hector was probably in that house.

Parr took a deep breath and stepped out of the car. There was a shotgun in the trunk, but he opted against it in case civilians were inside. Most of the dope dealers, even the ones making six figures a year, still lived with their parents.

The trunk also held a Kevlar vest and he thought for a moment about putting it on but decided against it. He was probably being watched from all sides right now. If they knew he was sporting a vest, they would only aim at his head.

He looked behind him at all the houses on the street, but when he got to the driveway, he didn't hesitate. If he did, they would see his fear and know he didn't have an army of officers waiting around the corner. He opened the chain-link fence, walked right up to the door, and knocked. He rang the doorbell a few seconds later and glued his eye to the peephole. He couldn't see into the house through the peephole, but he would be able to see light if no one was on the other side, looking out. He kept his eye on the light, and the second it went dark, he cocked up his leg and bashed his boot into the flimsy door.

Splinters rained down as the door slammed into the face of a Hispanic man in his twenties. The man grabbed his nose as blood began to flow. He tried to lift the sawed-off shotgun in his right hand. It was too late for Parr to go for his own sidearm, so he grabbed the shotgun. The barrel was pointed at his hip, and he twisted to the side just in time for the buckshot to spray behind him.

"Motherfucker!" the man yelled.

Grunting, Parr braced his legs and pushed back, slamming the man into the wall. He wrapped both hands around the handle of the shotgun and got his finger over the trigger. He pulled it, spraying another shot into the floor and loosening the man's grip with the recoil. Holding his finger under the trigger, he prevented another shot from being fired.

Parr spun with his elbow and it impacted against the man's nose and flung his head back. He landed a punch into his throat while his head was up, and the man gasped for air. Parr ripped away the shotgun and threw it behind him. He pulled out his Browning and pressed it into the man's left eye.

"You have ten seconds," Parr said, breathing hard. "I don't like what I hear, you die."

"Fuck you, *puto*."

He cocked back and slammed the butt of his gun into the man's nose. It crunched, and the blood that was already flowing erupted down his neck and chest. Parr flipped him to the ground onto his stomach. He put his knees into the man's back and lifted his chin with his palms, putting pressure on his spine. He lifted until the man screamed then lowered him.

"I lied. I won't kill you. I'll turn you into a fucking vegetable so you can lie in bed all day. You won't move. You won't talk or shit or eat. You'll just lie there." He lifted the man's chin again, evoking another scream. "You're Hector, right?" He lifted higher.

"Yeah," he gasped though his air was being cutting off.

"Good, now we're getting somewhere, Hector. Was it Mateo who told you I was comin' just now?"

"Yeah."

"Good, good. Few more questions and you'll never see me again. All right? But if you lie to me, I'm comin' back here. Not during the day, though. I'm going to sneak in here at night while you're sleeping, and I'm going to cut your guts out and feed 'em to you. Then I'm gonna cut up any other pricks in this house. I don't care if it's your daddy, your mommy, or your nana. You feelin' me?"

"Yeah, yeah, I feel you."

"Good. Now, where are the two keys you got off the body in the car that was burned up?"

"They downstairs."

"Where downstairs?"

"In a cabinet. You just go down and it's by the window."

"You merc that poor bastard I found?"

"No way, *ese*. I don't do that shit."

"Coulda fooled me with the shotgun you said hello with."

"That was for protection, man. I ain't never killed nobody. I just deal, man. That's it. I just want that paper. I ain't tryin' to get no life in prison."

"Let's pretend for a minute I believe you. Then who's responsible for that body?"

"It was a cop, man. A cop did that shit."

"See, now here's the problem: Mateo told me that a cop got paid off to tip you last time we were supposed to meet. So one of you is playing me for a bitch again, and that ain't the right move."

"Nah, man, it's the truth. Cop did that body, and then when the keys was gone, he got five G's when he ratted you out."

"What cop was it? Did you see him?"

"Nah. I talked to him on the phone."

"What was his name?"
"Jon, man. Jon something."
"Jon what?"
"Stanton."

13

Stanton went into police headquarters with Mindi. They marched down a long hallway with photographs of various high-ranking officers on the wall. Toward the end was a photo of the president and one of the attorney general. They got to a supply closet and Mindi opened the door. He followed her into a makeshift office that held a desk, chair, computer and a couple of filing cabinets. The supply closet still stank of cleaning products.

"It's not much," she said, "but it's yours. Orson said you would want something private and this is as private as it gets."

"It'll be fine. Thanks."

"So when do you want to go get Freddy?"

"I need to speak to a tech expert first."

"What kind?"

"Imagery, DVD specifically. Do you have one on site?"

"No, we contract with a company. Do you want to go out there?"

"Actually"—he pulled the blank disc out of the file—"can you head there and give them this?"

"What is it?"

"It's a disc I found in the Steeds' home. I think it may have had something on it that's been erased. Have them see if they can bring it up."

"All right, no prob. What are you going to do?"

"I need to speak with Orson for a bit."

"Okay. I'll be right back."

Stanton waited for her to leave then sat down. The carpet was stained so deeply he thought dark brown was its natural color, until he noticed splotches where it was clean beige. He took out his cell phone and dialed his ex-wife. His oldest, Matt, should've just finished a tennis lesson, and he wanted to ask him how it had gone. The call went straight to voicemail. He took a deep breath and rose to find Orson.

Although the headquarters served as a fully functioning precinct, equipped with holding cells and SWAT lockers, it still had the air of an administrative headquarters. He saw more office workers than field uniforms and it made him uneasy. He had never felt comfortable with the top brass. His only experiences with them had revealed pettiness and bureaucracy at best, and corruption at worst. He felt much more at home with the front-line cops.

Stanton hurried to Orson's office. Orson, who was on the phone at his desk, looked surprised to see him.

"I'll have to call you back." Orson hung up the phone and put his hands behind his head in a relaxed posture. "What's up, Jon?"

"Just wondering if you had a minute."

"For you? Anytime."

Stanton shut the door and sat down. "Why am I here, Orson? I know the stats. Crimes like this happen here every day. Even with their contribution money, the Steeds' murder couldn't be the top priority of the whole department."

"You don't think the murder of two prominent citizens should be our top priority?"

"I didn't say it *shouldn't* be. I said it *couldn't* be. Unless everything I know about how bureaucracies work is wrong, you'd want to underplay your hand on this and hope it goes away until it's solved. Bringing me in here's bound to get some press. You knew that."

"I did." He exhaled loudly and rubbed the bridge of his nose between his thumb and forefinger. "There's no other city like Las Vegas in the world, Jon. Not since ancient Rome has there been a place like ours. It's set up to cater to vice and nothing else. Nothing. So the people who provide that vice are the true governors. Hell, our mayor's a mob lawyer. That's our essence."

"You need to be straight with me."

"I know, I know. The thing is, the mayor, the sheriff, the city council—we don't run this place. We know who we really work for and that's the casinos." He pointed to a photo on his wall of him shaking hands with a man in a tuxedo. "You see that guy? That's Bill James. He owns more of this city now than Wynn, Trump or any of those others. He also happens to be the chief suspect in this case."

Stanton recognized him. He was in the Havana and had nearly knocked unconscious the other man that got dragged away. He decided not to mention it. "There was nothing in the file about him."

"No, there wouldn't be. He hasn't been officially mentioned. They were suing each other, or more specifically Daniel Steed was suing him. And not just a few million. The lawsuit was for billions. It would've bankrupted Bill James."

"Has he been questioned?"

"You kiddin' me? The county attorneys would have my ass. He's donated more to campaigns in this county than every other organization and individual combined. He knows how to grease the wheels."

"So you brought me in here to find evidence against him?"

Orson shook his head. "No, we didn't. The opposite actually. Bill James brought you in. He came to me and asked who the best investigator I've ever met was. I told him you were. He said to spare no expense and get you here. He's the one picking up your tab. He knows everybody thinks he did this. He wants his name cleared."

"You believe him?"

"I don't know. He comes from a different time, back when casino owners solved their problems with holes in the desert. And that would just be for stealing a few bucks in chips or cheating at craps. I can't imagine how far he would go to protect his entire fortune."

"You think I could talk to him?"

"Absolutely not. He wants no involvement in this. We're serious about that, Jon. Papers get ahold of that and they'll start painting him as the killer. You speak with him, and we'll have to have you on the next plane out of here. I really don't want that. I don't want any of this. I just want to find who did this and forget about this damned case."

Stanton rose. "I appreciate you being honest with me."

"Jon," he said as Stanton turned to leave, "never forget who the real bosses are here. As long as you do that, you won't step on any toes. That's how I get by."

Stanton shut the door behind him and left without responding.

14

Stanton waited in the office until six o' clock, but Mindi didn't make it back in time. He headed outside after stopping briefly at the front desk to ask where Marty was.

"Ain't seen him," the receptionist said without looking up from a form she was working on.

Las Vegas gave off warmth; an energy. Some feeling that other cities didn't have filled the air. Excitement maybe. Or perhaps despair.

It was Friday night and the weekends were the town's busiest nights.

He didn't feel like driving so he grabbed a cab. The young cabbie had a flattop and army tattoos on his forearms. He sped through a few parking lots, cut off cars, and had Stanton back on the Strip within minutes. Stanton tipped him well as he stepped out in front of the Luxor. The billboard up across the street advertised a strip club.

He didn't want to go back to his hotel yet so he went inside the Luxor. The Egyptian hieroglyphs and statues were truly awe inspiring. People walked past them without so much as a glance, yet they would have paid thousands of dollars to see the originals in Egypt. The only difference between the two were their ages.

The casino was designed like any other casino, but it was more open and the ceilings were higher. A black Lamborghini was placed on a lighted pedestal; a sign next to it proclaimed that it could be won for a one-dollar bet. Beyond that were television cameras pointed at a magician performing tricks for a crowd.

Stanton walked over and stood behind two drunken women in tight skirts. One of them looked at him and smiled, and he smiled back.

"You looking for a date?" she asked.

"No, just walking around."

She touched his chest. "If you change your mind I'll be in the bar."

The magician levitated inches off the ground, to the amazement of the crowd. Stanton instantly saw what was happening. The magician was wearing long pants and had his back turned to the crowd, exposing only his heels. He lifted himself on one foot, making sure that both heels were stuck together and that the other foot was flat and in the air. Gasps rippled through the crowd. It was a clever trick. The magician turned back around to applause and noticed Stanton.

"You, my friend. You think I can read your mind?"

Stanton shrugged.

"Does anyone here believe that one person can read another's mind?"

About half the people in the crowd raised their hands.

"For those of you nonbelievers, if I read the mind of a total stranger, would you believe?" He walked over to Stanton, holding a piece of paper in his hand. "I want you to think of an item —any item—right now. Get it in your mind and I'm going to draw it on this paper." The magician made some scribbles then lowered the paper.

The magician closed his eyes, his breathing slowed, and he touched Stanton lightly on the shoulder.

"What was your item?"

"A shark."

"Did you say a shark?"

"Yes."

The magician held up the paper, showing a drawing of a shark coming out of the water like the one on the posters for *Jaws*. The crowd cheered and clapped.

Stanton leaned in close to the magician and said, "I could see the lead tip on your finger."

The magician smiled, shrugged, and moved on to someone else. He had drawn the shark after Stanton said it, using the lead tip. With the paper lowered, no one should have noticed.

Stanton ambled around the casino a bit more then headed back outside. He was about to walk back to the Mirage when he remembered that the tram was nearby. Several blocks down he found an entrance, where he bought a ticket with his credit card. He caught the northbound tram and when he got on, he was alone.

The tram appeared to be clean, except for marker scribbles on the interior close to his seat. A route map over the doors showed which casinos were near which stops.

A voice over the speakers announced the next stop and the tram started with a jolt. It weaved in between buildings and over trees, neon lights glimmering just outside the windows. On the opposite side of the Strip, out a thousand yards or so, were the cheap motels and hostels.

At the Harrah's stop, two women and a man got on. They were middle-aged, perhaps in their late fifties, and drunk. The man had on a pinstripe suit, his shiny hair slicked back. He wore pinky rings on each hand and had a diamond stud in his ear. He had a hand on each woman and they were speaking softly to each other.

"I think it'd be hot if you two kissed," the man said.

They giggled then proceeded to kiss. Stanton looked out the windows, pretending not to pay attention.

"What the hell you lookin' at?"

He looked back to see the man staring right at him.

"I wasn't looking."

"The hell you weren't."

"Honey," one of the women said, "calm down."

"I asked you a question. What you lookin' at?"

Stanton felt like pulling out his badge and teaching him a lesson by making him get off the tram, searching him, forcing him to divulge information about himself, humiliating him, and making him feel powerless. But he fought the urge. Thoughts like that didn't come from a good place. The man wanted to feel powerful in front of the women. Stanton pitied him.

"I'm sorry you've taken offense. I was trying not to look."

"That's damn right you're sorry." A grin crossed his face. He turned to the women. "See, that's how you gotta treat people. Just grab 'em by the balls."

As the trio stumbled off the tram at the next stop, the man gave Stanton a quick glance and a smirk. Stanton got off near the Bellagio and got into the last car of a southbound tram.

He was out of the camera's view, where the man he was looking for would have sat. He stared at the empty seats in front of him, picturing Daniel and Emily Steed, the smiles on their faces, and the love between them. He could feel rage and hatred. It bubbled up in him and he knew what he would do, what he was there to do. He could feel the heaviness of the gun and the itchy promise of the woolen ski mask in his pocket. He knew they were going to die and they had no idea. He had absolute power over their lives, matched only by their parents, who had created them. He was their executioner. It was… exciting.

That's why you had an erection already, didn't you?

Stanton rose and went over to the spot where the man had stood. He lifted his arm toward the seats, reached over, and pulled as if grabbing someone by the hair. He held that person bent over with one hand and fired a gun with the other. Looking up at his reflection in the windows, Stanton saw the exact posture the unknown subject had been in. He examined every inch of floor and window as well as outside. He looked behind him. The tram slowed and came to a stop as the voice announced the Flamingo and Caesar's Palace—the stop where the unsub would have exited. Stanton stepped off the tram and saw an elevator and stairs. He didn't want to take the elevator. It was only a short ride one floor down, but he would be trapped there. Right now, he felt like flying.

He ran to the stairs and took them two at a time, pretending to pull off a ski mask and tucking away the gun. On the first floor, he attempted to act normal, to fit in. He glanced around.

People would be coming into the terminal there. Having other people so near was exciting. The tram rumbled past overhead, two bodies slumped in its seats. Stanton watched the tram, following it, and watched other people's reactions to it. But they didn't see it, not like he did. In that way, he had power over *them*, too.

He continued out of the terminal and arrived at a narrow corridor of concrete. This was a prison. The walls closed in on him. He was a Titan, and the walls were crushing him. His excitement was fading. The tingling in his belly, the fire in his brain and the racing of his heart... it was all leaving as he re-entered the world out on the street corner.

A woman walked past him by herself. She held tightly to her purse when she saw him. Stanton looked around. It was secluded and dark. No one within fifty or sixty feet...

He watched the woman as she entered the terminal. Who was she to him? How dare she walk by him without acknowledging his greatness. The great deeds he had just performed? The acts that so few others had the guts to do?

The excitement was back. He was just behind the Flamingo on Winnick Avenue. No one was around to help. The unsub would have had to run somewhere.

Where would you go?

Stanton walked past a building with no clear name or purpose then saw the Hilton vacation suites at the Flamingo. It was his first sight of civilization since he'd gotten off the tram. He went to the front desk where a security guard was sitting off to the right, reading a magazine and surfing the Internet at the same time. There was a half-eaten sandwich on the desk in front of him.

"Excuse me," Stanton said, "I need a list of all the crimes that were reported here on June twelfth, just after ten at night."

15

As Alma Parr walked into the Metro PD headquarters, he glanced up at the two palm trees on either side of the entrance. An empty beer bottle had been thrown up into one of them and he stood under the tree, looking up at the bottle. Briefly, he thought it would be amusing if he shot it down. Instead, he picked up a rock and threw it at the bottle. He missed twice before nailing it, sending it crashing to the pavement below. He picked up the large pieces and threw them in a trash bin outside the building.

The precinct was busy—it was always busy—and he still wasn't used to it. The new building now housed the headquarters of Robbery-Homicide. He remembered driving past the location as a beat cop when it was nothing but an empty lot.

"Captain," one of the secretaries said as she hurried up next to him, "I need to speak to you about that Antonsens case."

"Who is that again?"

"The flasher we interviewed last week for the robbery of the Laundromat on Maryland."

"Right," he said, stopping at the soda machine and checking the change in his pocket. "What about him?"

"He says he's filing a lawsuit for, um—how did he put it? —'lighting him up.'"

He grinned. "I don't think that's what you mean. Lighting him up means I shot him. I didn't shoot him. He's claiming I kicked his ass."

"Yeah, well, that. He says he's suing us, and he wants you to call his lawyer."

"If he was actually gonna sue us, he would just do it." He put a dollar in the machine and selected an energy drink. "He's just threatening a suit to have me call some meth-head acting as his lawyer. Ignore it."

"Are you sure? I think the in-house counsel would think that we should—"

"Candace, I'm telling you, forget about it. It'll just go away."

"If you say so."

"Anything else?"

"A woman named Jessica called twice, and somebody from the Special Operations Division called about that burn victim in the car."

He turned to her now. "What'd they say?"

"Um, hold on... oh, here it is. Sorry, new phone. Um, they said that the car was registered to a Rudy Henti out of San Bernardino, California. They haven't been able to find him. All the numbers and addresses they had for him were invalid. They ran his social security card for employment, and the last entry said he was deported two years ago."

"Huh. That's too bad. All right. Anything else?"

"Nothing pressing. You do have about ten messages on your phone."

"I'll get to them," he said, walking away down the hall.

"Alma—"

"I'll get to them. I promise."

Parr walked down the hall and bumped fists with one of his detectives, Parsons, then stopped briefly to speak with Javier. He asked him to grab Jay and come to his office.

Parr went into his office and sat down. Behind him was a large framed movie poster for *Scarface*, depicting Al Pacino sitting at his desk, a cigar in his mouth. A football signed by Dick Butkus rested on a shelf, and he looked at it for a second before Javier knocked and came in. He lay on the couch and put his feet up while Jay sat down in a chair and threw a file on the desk in front of him. It was marked JON STANTON: CONFIDENTIAL.

"Was it hard to get?" Parr asked, opening the file.

"Not really," Jay said. "IAD in San Diego hates his guts and gave it up after a couple phone calls and a promise to destroy it afterwards. They're not originals, obviously."

"Shot by his partner," Javier said. "Dude was in the hospital over a month. His heart stopped twice. Tough son of a bitch."

"Or just lucky," Parr said, reading through the commendations and citations Stanton had received during his time on the force.

"I got a weird vibe from him," Jay said. "It was like I was at my shrink."

"Since when do you see a shrink?"

"Family therapist. Marcy thought it would help with our issues." He leaned back in the chair. "How's Jessica? When you guys settling down?"

"I broke up with her," Parr said, not taking his eyes off the file.

"What? I thought you guys were talking wedding bells?"

"Marriages and this job don't mix." He flipped through a couple pages in the file. "He doesn't have a single brutality or excessive force complaint."

"So what?"

"So how many cops you know don't have a single one? Even the squeaky cleans got one or two against them. He doesn't have any."

"What does that mean?"

"I don't know. I think it means he's either a pussy or smart as shit." He closed the file. "Something's off about him. No one gets a doctorate and works homicide for fifty grand a year. Especially when you got a wife and kids at home."

"He got divorced," Javier said. "The file hasn't been updated."

"How'd you hear that?"

"Mindi told us."

"What the hell does she have to do with this?"

"Nothin'. She was just curious. Said she was helpin' him out and just came down and hung out for a while."

"Keep her away from anything sensitive. I don't trust her."

"She's harmless."

"Just do what I say."

Jay asked, "What about Jon?"

"Fucker's smart. He'll see a tail. But I want eyes on him."

"We could pull somebody from Homeland Security detail. Those guys can tail the president without being seen."

"That's not a bad idea. I'll put in the word and see if anything turns up. For now, though, I need someone in San Diego to get out on the streets and beat the bushes a little. See if anyone knows anything about Stanton. If he's crooked, this can't be the first time."

Jay shrugged. "I can go, I guess."

"Javier, you okay with him gone for a few days?"

"Yeah, it'll give me and Mrs. Jay Reed a chance to catch up."

"Fuck you," Jay said. "Like she'd touch your wetback ass."

"Don't knock it till you try it, holmes. This is twelve inches of python right here."

Parr smirked. "If your brains were as big as your cock maybe you'd actually close some fucking cases."

Javier shrugged and rose off the couch. "Anything else, *Jefe*? I got me a lunch date."

"Don't tell anybody about this. I want to keep it between us for now. I hear Stanton's tight with Orson, and I don't need him on my ass right now."

Javier nodded. "I'll see you guys when I see you."

Jay rose to leave as well, and Parr said, "Hang on a sec."

"Yeah?"

"Remember Antonsen? That flasher prick who robbed a Laundromat then exposed himself to some kids who were there?"

"Yeah," he said, chuckling. "What about him?"

"Said he wants to sue us."

"No shit?"

"No shit. I want you to go pay him a visit and change his mind."

"How hard should I change his mind?"

"Really fucking hard. He's connected to that flasher-pedophile bullshit community. He'll get the word out that we don't fuck around."

"You got it. Anything else?"

"Jon Stanton might actually solve this thing. If he does, it's gonna make us look like monkeys. Make sure he doesn't."

16

Stanton went down to the Sunday morning buffet. The food was laid out nicely and the dishes were freshly washed. He piled eggs and watermelon onto his plate before grabbing a Diet Coke and sitting down at a table by the window.

He'd spent the previous day doing little. Most of the Robbery-Homicide division, as well as Marty and Mindi, were off, and little work was expected from anyone there. He had met resistance at the Flamingo while trying to get a record of the crimes reported on June twelfth, and he didn't want to pull out a badge from San Diego. He had left a message for Marty, asking him to go down there and get it.

Stanton's cell phone buzzed. It was Mindi.

"Hey," he said. "How was your day off?"

"Sorry about that. That's like my only day off the whole week, and I didn't want to—"

"No, I was genuinely asking. It's all right."

"Oh, it was good. I spent time with my mom and went shopping. She lives in Portland but gets down here every couple of months. What'd you do?"

"I watched the *Beatles Love* show. Other than that, I just walked around. Went to the mall and bought a few things for my boys."

"Aw, cute. Do you miss them?"

"I do. I haven't been able to spend as much time with them since the divorce." Stanton dipped some eggs in ketchup and took a bite. "So what's going on?"

"I was just calling to see if you wanted to go see Fredrick Steed today."

"Not today."

"Why not?"

"It's Sunday."

"Yeah, and?"

"It's the Sabbath."

There was a pause on the other line. "You're kidding, right?"

"No, I don't work on the Sabbath."

"Wow. Never heard that in this town before. So what're you gonna do?"

"I'm going to church."

"What church?"

He took another bite of eggs. "There's one nearby on North Hollywood. Why? Do you want to join me?"

She hesitated. "Sure."

"I was kind of kidding. There's no pressure."

"No, maybe I can talk you into speaking about the case. What time?"

"Half an hour."

"I'll pick you up."

Stanton hung up and finished his eggs. Perhaps he'd been wrong about Mindi. She seemed genuinely interested in solving this and offered little of the duplicitous behavior he'd seen with people trying to rise in government careers.

Before leaving, he put his plate in a bin by the garbage and thanked the two Hispanic men who were serving. He walked once around the casino in a slow, purposeful manner. For some reason he couldn't identify, he was fascinated with the gamblers. It was early in the morning but they were still here. Stanton stopped at a table and stood alongside a group of them, watching their movements, their eyes, and their facial expressions. They took deep drags off cigarettes and snuffed them out prematurely, only to light more. They sipped their beers if they were losing then guzzled them if they were winning.

An older man with a graying wisp of a beard held a lit cigarette between his fingers and another in his mouth. He forgot the one in his mouth was there and took a sip of a cocktail, dipping the cigarette into it. He didn't notice until the dealer said something. The man swore, placed the cigarette on an ashtray, and finished the drink.

Working memory, the memory a person is using at any given time, could only hold half a dozen objects. When a new object or information presents itself, like a dangling cigarette, it pushes another object out of the working memory. The gamblers had such focus, were so completely engrossed in the games, that their brains were literally not functioning normally. Their amygdala could not bring a new object into the working memory. They were more or less zombies.

Stanton went outside and felt the sunshine. The balminess from the pavement wafted up and warmed him. He saw Mindi sitting in a Jeep Wrangler, waiting for him. As he approached, she leaned over and opened the door.

"I like the Jeep," he said.

"Thanks. It's my baby. I've had it since college."

Stanton went to strap in and found there wasn't a seatbelt. "Not the safest car."

"No, but that's not why people get Jeeps." She pulled out of the Mirage and onto Las Vegas Boulevard. "Never been to a Mormon church before."

"Almost the same as anywhere else."

"I'm not nervous."

"You're clicking the nails on your thumb and pointer finger. I can hear it from here."

She stopped. "You don't miss anything, do you?"

They drove in silence for a few minutes then flipped the radio to a classic rock station. The DJ discussed his bowel movement that morning.

"Sorry," she said, changing the station.

"It's fine."

"Can I ask you something personal, Jon?"

"Sure."

"Why did you come out here? It seems like this is the last place someone like you would want to be."

"Someone like me?"

"That came out wrong. But you know what I mean. This place... even the cops..."

"I know. But Orson's been good to me for a long time. He asked a favor and I did it."

"Huh. So what do you think so far? You've got to have some impressions about who we're looking for."

Stanton looked out the window as Mindi drove up a ramp onto the freeway. "I was investigating a case once, like, fifteen years ago. I'd only been on the force a couple of years and was basically doing DUIs and traffic tickets like everybody else. I'd gotten some reports of a drunk driver hitting a lamppost and taking off, so I went down there. I got a call from someone at the precinct, letting me know they'd stopped the guy three miles from where I was, and they were transporting him back for interrogation and booking.

"So, I spoke to a couple of witnesses and got statements and headed back to the precinct. We had this interrogation room that was really more like a closet that we'd taken over 'cause we ran out of room. You had to go through two doors to go into it. They told me where he was, to go interview him, and to ask for his consent to take his blood. I went through the first door... and I stopped. I just completely stopped and couldn't move. It felt cold, and there was this gnawing in my gut. It felt tight, like I'd eaten something bad and was about to vomit. And this feeling just came over me about this guy. I'd never met him, never talked to him, but I had this feeling about him.

"I went in, and he seemed like a normal guy. Had an Eastern European accent. He consented to the blood draw, so I took his statement and sent in a phlebotomist and didn't think about him again. About a month later, I found out from one of the other detectives that he'd been arrested on a warrant out of Los Angeles that was issued by proxy for the International Criminal

Court. He had been a soldier during the Bosnian War, stationed at a camp in Foca, where his job, his literal job, was to rape young girls and women every day. He was extradited and convicted. The court found that he was responsible for at least four hundred rapes and over a dozen murders.

"What I felt was evil. Real evil. Not DUIs and pot possession and all the other things we deal with every day. You can feel evil. It's an entity. I get the same feeling from whoever did this."

"Wow. That is not what I thought you would say."

"What'd you think I'd say?"

"That he's six feet tall and has a prison record or something."

Stanton grinned.

They got off the freeway a block from the church. The brown-brick building had a spire, and the parking lot was full. Mindi parked in a space across the street, and they walked inside. It was well lit, with a painting of Jesus Christ in the foyer. They took their seats in the large auditorium where the sacrament meeting was held. The Mormon equivalent of mass.

When it was over and Stanton turned his phone back on, he saw he had a voicemail. It was Marty asking him to call right away. "Marty just called and said he has an emergency."

"You want me to call him?"

"No, I got it," he said, dialing the number.

There was no answer and it went to voicemail.

17

Bill James stepped off the plane in Havana, Cuba, and stood for a moment on the mobile staircase, inhaling the salty air. It'd been too long since he'd been here. Cuba had a way of freshening his soul. If only the damn Communists would go away he could buy a home and retire there, then find a nice, young Cuban girl and have several children in his late sixties. Not having children had always been his biggest regret.

A car was waiting for him. It wasn't a limo or even a Lincoln Town Car, but an old Buick that looked as though it belonged in the 1960s. That was the thing about Cuba: it hadn't progressed a single day since the revolution. The moment capitalism ended, so did its forward momentum.

"*Hola*," he said to the driver.

"*Hola.*"

"English?"

"*Si.*"

"Is Salvatore meeting me in person?"

"*Si.*"

James nodded as he looked at the backseat of the car. For every meeting he had ever had with Salvatore, he placed his chances of surviving the encounter at around ninety percent. Right now, he wasn't sure if his odds were that high.

He got into the backseat and the driver pulled away from the tarmac. The vegetation surrounding the airport was something out of a jungle movie, and almost nothing obstructed the views of the city and mountains. The ocean wasn't far off and he looked forward to spending some time fishing. After reading Hemingway's words about fishing in Cuba as a teenager, he'd been hooked ever since. When he finally had the opportunity to really do it, he wasn't disappointed. The sea was calm, the beer didn't stop flowing, the old fisherman he had chartered the boat from had fascinating story after fascinating story, and the sky was open and blue. It was, as far as he could recall, the greatest time of his life.

He pulled out a Graham Greene novel from the one suitcase he had brought with him and began to read. He glanced up after he had read five chapters and saw that they had arrived in downtown Havana. It was a unique city, where pristine churches that could've been torn out of the Middle Ages mingled with modern, pre-revolution office buildings and beautifully designed amphitheaters and hotels.

But there was another side to the city. James saw it in the eyes of its inhabitants as he rode past them. There was hatred there, unfocused and wild, like a rampant energy shooting out of them. These people stood on the corners, much as their counterparts did in the States. They huddled in the filthy back alleys, fifty men waiting to rob anyone foolish enough to go down there alone. They sat on porches hoping for jobs that would never come. They stood on sidewalks watching people walk by; not out of curiosity, but because they simply had absolutely nothing else to do.

"You look good," the driver said, turning at an intersection and nearly running over a man on a bike. "Skinny and tan."

"Have we met?"

He laughed. "My name is Roberto. I was a child last time you were here. I used to shine shoes for Mr. Salvatore. Now I drive his cars. Soon, I will do more."

"How old are you?"

"Seventeen."

They pulled up to the front of the Santa Isabel. James had always thought it was not only the finest hotel in the city, but perhaps the finest building in the city. It was built in the eighteenth century and had required little renovation since. It overlooked the entire city and, more importantly, the Plaza de Armas.

James got out and walked through the massive double doors. He waved away bellhops and greeters. He knew where he had been summoned to go. The building had elevators but he never trusted them. He avoided Communist workmanship at all costs, especially if his life was on the line. He remembered visiting the Soviet Union during the height of the Cold War. He was smuggling in grain at a four hundred percent profit. He'd asked one of his distributors there what life was like. "We pretend to work," the man had said, "and they pretend to pay us."

The climb to the top floor took a while, and about halfway up, he stopped and sat in a leather armchair in the stairwell, looking out gothic windows at the city below. When he had caught his breath, he continued to the top floor.

The suite took up almost the entire top floor. Of the floor's twelve rooms, Salvatore was leasing ten of them on a month-to-month basis. James went all the way to the end of the hall and looked out the window at the fountain in the courtyard below before he knocked on the door.

A woman in a white tank top and white workout pants answered. Her bright blonde hair was pulled back. She was obviously American or British.

"I'm here to see Jorge."

"You must be William," she said, extending her hand. "I'm Celeste."

"Nice to meet you," he said, shaking her hand, "and please, call me Bill."

She turned and walked inside and he followed, shutting the door behind him. The suite was massive, far larger than his suite at the hotel in Vegas. At least a dozen windows looked out in every direction, and a hot tub took up one of the smaller guest rooms to the side. The furniture was all leather, and fresh flowers graced every table. A breeze was blowing in through the balcony's double doors. James could see Jorge on the balcony, sitting at a table with another man arguing about something.

Jorge was wearing a white Polo sweater with white pants and leather shoes with no socks. Aviator sunglasses were pushed up into his hair. Though the outfit probably cost at least two or three thousand dollars, James thought he looked like everything else in the country: antiquated.

Jorge saw him and smiled. He curtly dismissed his other guest and waved for James to join him outside. The other man walked in, hat in hand, a defeated expression on his face, and averted his eyes from James.

Jorge stood up and hugged James as he stepped outside. He kissed James on both cheeks then offered him a seat across from him.

"How are you, my friend?" he said in his thick, grainy voice with the hint of a European education.

"I'm doing well. How you been?"

"I apparently have an ulcer."

"You're kidding? You're thirty-five, aren't you? What are you doing with an ulcer?"

He shook his head. "This damn business. If it's not my competitors, it's the police. If it's not the police, it's the courts, the administrators, or the party chairs... the mouths you have to feed just to do business here never stop."

"You're rich enough. You could just hang it all up and retire to some beach somewhere."

"You can never be rich enough. It's always right there, right on the edge." He snapped his fingers. "In a single moment, you can go from being a rich man to being a poor one."

"I suppose that's true enough. Congratulations on your wedding, by the way."

"You should be getting the invitation in the next few months."

"How's your mother?" he asked, barely able to suppress a grin.

"She's doing well. She talks about you sometimes. She says she made a mistake and you should've been the one she married."

"I can't honestly say that I haven't thought that same thing."

Jorge took a deep breath and leaned back in the chair, looking out over the city. "What's this I hear about the board not approving the acquisition?"

"It's a minor setback."

"It doesn't sound minor."

"It is. It's one person on the board stirring up doubts in everyone else. If I can convince him—or more likely, pay him off—I think the rest of the board will fall in line."

"What if you cannot convince him or, like you said, pay him off?"

"I will."

"I have four hundred million of my family's money invested in this, William. If this acquisition does not go through in time —"

"I give you my word, Jorge—it will go through."

Jorge stared at him, unwavering. His eyes were cold and black. James had seen those eyes make heartless, calculated decisions as coolly as if he were ordering a cocktail. Jorge's face finally broke into a smile.

"Okay, I trust you, William. I know you will take care of this for me."

"I will."

"Good. Now you must stay in Havana tonight. I will get you women. We will go out and get the best drugs and not sleep until tomorrow."

James chuckled. "That's a young man's territory and I'm not a young man. If it's all right with you, I think I'll just hit the sack early tonight and go fishing tomorrow."

"Fishing?" He shook his head in disbelief. "You are only old if you act old. You know that, do you not?"

"Maybe. But I still really want to go fishing."

Jorge stood, and James followed suit. They hugged, and Jorge kissed him again.

"Do not disappoint me, William. I am very fond of you."

"I won't."

As James left the suite, a trickle of fear ran down his spine. *I'm very fond of you.* James knew it wasn't a compliment. It was a message: you are expendable.

18

Alma Parr stood on Las Vegas Boulevard in a sports coat and jeans. Wide black sunglasses covered his eyes and sweat slicked the back of his thick neck. He leaned against a pole, watching people—mostly illegal Hispanics who found it difficult to find other work—hand out flyers for hookers and pornography. Even a few women were doing it. It was part of the cityscape, like the buildings, casinos, and restaurants. He wouldn't have noticed if not for the child standing nearby.

The child, a boy of no more than twelve or thirteen, finished the hot dog he was eating, rose, and said something to a man who was handing out flyers. The man took off the vest he was wearing, which contained all the material, and put it around the boy who began to hand out flyers as the man walked away.

Parr looked down both sides of the street then crossed it. A large black SUV blared its horn, and Parr stood in the middle of the street, staring through the windshield, waiting for the driver to lean out the window and say something. Instead, the man rolled up his window. Parr continued across the street.

"*Hola*," he said.

"*Hola.*"

"*Habla ingles?*"

"No."

"Yes you do. I've seen you here before. I've seen you talk to some of the customers."

The boy looked down at his feet.

"What's your name?" Parr asked.

"Carlito."

"Carlito. I like that name. Like *Carlito's Way*. You seen that movie?"

The boy's face lit up. "*Si*. I see on TV and watch many times. Al Pacino is best actor."

"He's my favorite, too. You look up to Carlito in that movie, don't you?"

"*Si.*"

"Let me ask you, would Carlito be on this corner handing out pictures of asses to old ladies walking by?"

The boy thought a moment. "No."

"No. Then why are you?"

"I have to make money. My mom no work."

"There are other ways to make money." Parr glanced around. Usually, the younger kids doing this had handlers close by who checked up on them every hour or so. "How much money do you make doing this?"

"One dollar an hour."

"How many hours do you work?"

"Four hours."

"Every day?"

"*Si.*"

"So that's twenty-eight dollars in one week?"

"*Si.*"

Parr took out his wallet. "Carlito, I have two hundred and sixteen dollars in my wallet. That's all the cash I have. That's almost eight weeks of work for you."

"*Si.*"

"Okay, well, I want you to take this money, but I'm not giving it to you. Do you understand? I'm buying something with this money. This gives you two months that you don't have to work. In that time, the four hours you spend every day here, I want you to take just two of those hours and look for a good job. A job you can be proud of. *Sabes lo que estoy hablando*?"

"*Si*, I understand."

"Okay, here's the money. Do you promise that you'll hold up

your end of the deal?"

"*Si, gracias.*"

"*Eres bienvenido.*"

Parr watched the boy run off, a large smile on his face. The boy tucked the cash quickly into his pocket, making sure no one around him saw it. Parr heard a car horn across the street. There was a van parked where he had been standing. He dashed across the street before the next wave of cars came then he hopped into the passenger side of the van.

"What's up, brother?" the driver said.

"Shit, Danny, you still got that nasty beard?"

"Spend two months, twelve hours a day in this van, listening to the cocksuckers I listen to, and then lecture me about my appearance."

"Smells in here."

"Again, please refer to the previous comment. You look fuckin' huge. You on the juice?"

"No man, I told you, I play it clean. That stuff'll make your dick fall off."

He chuckled. "Heard you gettin' promoted soon?"

"Yeah? Where'd you hear that?"

"Told you, all I do in here is listen."

"What they got you doing anyway? I can't imagine Homeland Security's very busy in the casinos."

"You'd be surprised how many extremists come through this city. See, they're all hypocrites. They proclaim their love of Allah, wanting to destroy us, but they stop here and order a blow job and some coke at the hotel. Vegas is the first stop on the way to hell."

"Nice. Didn't know you were a poet."

"Among other things. So what'd you need?"

"What makes you think I need anything?"

"Don't call me in three months and then out of the blue you need to meet me right away? Unless you've become gay and want a date, you need something from me. So let's have it."

"Keep your panties on, princess. It's just a small favor."

"What kind of favor?"

"There's somebody I need surveillance on."

"You got a team."

"I know, but those two dipshits couldn't tail a blind man. I need somebody good for this. The mark's smart. He's also experienced and well trained."

He nodded and lit a cigarette. "Cop, huh?"

"It is what it is."

"What'd he do?"

"I don't know yet. That's why I need you."

"Well, at least tell me what I'm looking for."

"He was implicated in a homicide—that body in the burned car that we can't identify."

"Holy shit? That case? I saw that on the news. They pulled out the dude's teeth so you couldn't identify him after he was fried. That was awesome."

"It wasn't so awesome if you had to be there to peel him off the seats."

"You think this cop did that?"

"I don't know. I got my doubts, but I gotta follow up on it."

"You want round-the-clock?"

"Yeah."

He whistled. "That ain't cheap, my muscle-head friend. I'd have to get my guys pay and a half."

"I'll come up with the money."

"How?"

"I don't know. I'll get someone to approve it. Let me worry about that. I just need you to start as soon as possible. Tonight would be best."

"Who's the mark?"

"Jon Stanton. He's a detective from San Diego here as Orson's pet for a few weeks."

"You really think he did this?"

"I don't know. But if he did he's one dangerous shithead. Make sure your boys are packing and vested up."

19

Stanton checked his messages first thing when he woke Monday morning. Nothing from Marty. There was one message from Orson, asking if he wanted to go golfing that day, and one from Mindi saying she had a hit on Fredrick Steed's home address. There was another from his son, speaking in whispered tones, wishing him good night.

He dialed his ex's number and no one answered. He hung up without leaving a message. Next, he called Mindi's number and she answered on the second ring. He could hear a shower running in the background.

"Hey, Jon. You get my message?"

"Yeah. How'd you find him?"

"Found a case in the statewide. He's still on probation for a robbery charge. And you should see the rest of his history."

"Any sex offenses or burglaries?"

"No sex offenses. Don't remember if I saw any burglaries. Why?"

"Most sex offenders start off as burglars. When they enter a home and find someone asleep, they commit their first sexual assault and get a taste for it."

"Really? I thought they started out with sex offenses."

"Sometimes, but not usually."

"Well, I'll go grab his file and come get you. The place he's staying at is like an hour outside the city, so we should leave now. I should probably tell you, though, I Googled it, and it's, like, a weird commune. Like... a white supremacist compound or something."

"I don't think we should go alone, then."

"We're cops. What are they gonna do?"

Stanton grinned. Her innocence had its charm. "A lot. I'll talk to Orson and get some backup."

"I really don't think we need it. And that'll take a bunch of time. Let's just head out there."

"That's a bad idea. We'll get some backup from Orson. It shouldn't take more than an hour or two to get approved."

"All right, you're the boss here, I guess. I'll see ya at the precinct."

He placed the phone down on the side table and crawled up on the bed. There was a long cylindrical pillow lying there, made of a fluffy crimson material that was soft against his skin. He leaned his head back on it and flipped on the television. It was on a channel playing an infomercial for acne cream, but he didn't bother to change it. He wasn't watching for entertainment. Sometimes, he just needed background noise while he thought, fooling him into thinking he wasn't alone.

The video replayed in his mind. Professor Hoffman, his dissertation advisor, once had him run through memory studies as part of the psychology department's colloquium on modern mnemonic techniques. The premise was that they would teach an average student—Stanton, in this case—mnemonic techniques that could advance his recall. At the time of the study, no memory system ever developed had been statistically validated in any significant way. As Hoffman liked to say, they were selling psychological snake oil.

But Hoffman, one of the foremost memory experts in the United States, had stumbled upon a book on the history of ancient Greece while browsing the library. There was a section on Simonides of Ceos. During a party he was attending with over seventy other people, the roof of the home collapsed. Everyone was buried inside and Simonides was the sole survivor. When help arrived, they needed assistance finding the victims in the palatial home. Simonides, the story said, was able to recall exactly where every single guest had been when the roof fell.

Hoffman discovered that the ancient Greeks had a highly developed system of mnemonics associating concrete memories with those that would stand out. As he followed the thread to ancient Rome, he discovered politicians who were said to recite entire speeches lasting hours directly from memory. The ancients, or so he believed, had something that we had lost.

The associations were simple. One could have a house, a tent, a field, or anywhere that person liked. He would place the thing he wanted to remember with something so out of the ordinary that he was bound to remember its outrageousness and, hence, the object he wanted to recall, as well. Hoffman gave an example of being out on the town with his wife when he saw a horse-drawn carriage riding past. Realizing his anniversary was coming up, he wanted to remember the phone number on the side of the carriage without writing it down so that his wife would not notice. He thought of a home he remembered from the past, ran upstairs, and placed a horse in a bedroom. Next to the horse, he conjured a duck—for whatever reason, he had found ducks funny as a child—and painted the phone number in bright-red lettering on the horse. For extra effect, he imagined fireworks going off just outside the window. He remembered the phone number, even thirty-five years later.

After choosing Stanton for the study to be presented to the colloquium, Hoffman found that Stanton had perfect recall without the use of his new memory system, down to the number of women's earrings in a high school class photo that he had seen only for a few seconds.

Stanton had read about eidetic memory as a graduate student but found it indefinable. How could he tell if he was recalling something perfectly or if he was only perceiving it as being recalled perfectly? Stanton had noticed one trait in himself, though, that he didn't see in other officers: everything stayed with him. Ten years after visiting the scene of a homicide at a hotel, he could recall how many sticks of gum were left in the pack lying on the side table, what the thermostat had been set to, and... the exact expression on the corpse. Detectives in Homicide called it the "glamour shot," the final facial expression at the time of death. He remembered every glamour shot from every victim he had ever seen. Sometimes, in quiet moments, they came to him. He would close his eyes but they would be right there, seemingly between his eyes and eyelids. He was unable to shake them and would have to tolerate them until they went away on their own.

Stanton sat up in bed. He grabbed his phone and dialed Orson.

"Jon, what's goin' on?"

"Hey, I have a quick favor to ask."

"Anything."

"I need to pay Marty a visit and make sure he's okay. You think I could get his address?"

"Sure. Hey, you shoulda come out to the green yesterday. I left you a message but you never called me back."

"Sorry about that. I've been preoccupied with this."

"That's why I chose you, I guess. I'll have someone at the office text you the address."

"Thanks."

The address never came. He had to call the station several times and they had to confirm it with Orson before finally sending it. When it came an hour later, Stanton left the room. As he walked down the hallway, he heard a couple arguing behind closed doors. They were fighting because the man had not been honest about how the woman had looked in a dress she had worn the previous night. Apparently, he'd complimented her the entire night then made a comment the next morning about the dress not fitting well. Stanton grinned, remembering similar fights with his ex. He wished he'd known then what he knew now. It was all so trivial, but in the heat of the moment it had seemed so important. If he could go back he would apologize every time, his fault or not, and always have a soft heart with her.

He suddenly remembered that he hadn't talked to his kids in a few days, and he dialed the number as he rode the elevator down to the lobby.

A man answered. "Hello?"

"Is Melissa there?"

"Who's this?"

"This is Jon Stanton."

"Oh. She ain't here."

"Are Mathew and—"

The man hung up. Stanton sat on the line a moment then put away his phone. That must have been the football player. Lately, Melissa only dated athletes. If that was her type, he wondered why she had married him.

Stanton exited the elevators and the hotel without noticing anything around him. The valet brought out the Cadillac.

The address was twenty-seven minutes away, according to the GPS, and he made two wrong turns before getting onto the correct freeway. He finally turned onto Flower Avenue and found the three-bedroom rambler belonging to Marty. There was no car parked outside, and the blinds were drawn. He parked in the driveway and went up to the front door. He knocked then rang the doorbell. The other homes in the neighborhood looked almost identical, just different enough to add a bit of variety.

Stanton stepped back onto the front yard and looked around. Around back, he peered over the fence. All the blinds were drawn there as well. He was about to leave when he saw someone looking out a slit in the blinds on the front window. As soon as Stanton turned his head to look directly at the window, the slit closed.

He put his hand on his firearm, ensuring that it was there, a habit he had been taught by Sherman. Stanton knew the real reason they did this was for the sense of power that it gave them.

Stanton pounded on the door and shouted, "Police. Open up."

No response. He went to the garage door and tried to lift it but it was too heavy. He ran to the front and pushed. The thick door was locked with a deadbolt. He ran around the house and hopped the fence into the backyard. The backdoor was flimsy. He considered ramming through it, but he saw the basement window already had a massive chunk missing. He walked over and kicked the frame lightly on the side, shattering the glass. He cleared away the jagged edges with his shoe and crawled into the house.

The home was dark and smelled of mildew. It was stagnant, as if no one lived there or whoever did walked on eggshells in order not to disturb anything. Even the carpet had a coating of dust over vacuum cleaner tracks. As he passed a large, antique mirror on the south wall, Stanton glanced in the mirror, almost expecting to see someone else there.

There were three doors: one on the south wall, one on the east, and one on the north. The door to the north was open, leading upstairs. He peered up the stairs. Taking a few steps out, he looked straight up to see if anybody was standing at the railing above. No one was there.

Stanton took each step slowly, almost gingerly, as if he were walking on broken glass. He was halfway up the steps when he heard boots on linoleum and the turning of a lock.

"Police!"

He bolted toward the sound just in time to see the back of someone sprinting out of the backdoor. Stanton dashed down the hallway. He saw the figure, who was wearing a ski mask, hop the fence into the neighbor's yard. Stanton sprinted after him and dove over the fence. The man was heading straight for the back porch and the door that led inside the house.

Stanton considered firing at him, but he didn't know if civilians were inside. Instead, he landed hard on his feet from the jump over the fence and began running again. The man tried the backdoor, which was locked. He looked back at Stanton then rushed around the house and over the chain-link fence.

Stanton did the same, following the man down the sidewalk to an office park. He didn't take his eyes off him for a second, not even to look at the cars speeding toward him as he crossed the street.

The man was fast but he was slowing down. He was wearing what looked like work boots and they didn't help his endurance.

Stanton was at a full sprint now, breathing hard. He tasted bile in his mouth as his wind left him and his side began to ache. The man suddenly bolted right, down an alley, and Stanton trailed him. He opened a side door to a building and ran inside. Stanton ran in after him.

It was an industrial kitchen. Two massive ovens took up both sides of the room. Between them was an island with a countertop cluttered with dishes, food and cutlery. He could hear voices in the next room, just past a thick plastic door. Stanton held his firearm low.

He walked slowly around the island, his eyes glued to the door in front of him. He glanced down at the cupboards. They were too small for someone to hide in. To his right was a large metal freezer door with a latch on it. He reached for the latch, then heard the crash of pots and pans behind him.

Stanton spun around, his eyes fixed in the direction of the sound. Gun first, he moved toward it. When he rounded the island, he saw two frying pans on the floor. As he moved toward the pans, boots stomped up behind him. He turned just in time to see a figure swing a pipe at him.

The impact was deafening. His eyes slammed shut and watered. He tasted blood pouring out of his mouth and nostrils. His lips ached and began to swell. He lifted his gun, but the man tackled him and they both went down. Stanton tried to lift him enough to free his arm but the figure struck again with the pipe and nailed him in the ribs, knocking the wind out of him. Stanton was reaching for the backup .38 revolver tucked in a holster at his ankle when he felt another impact across his jaw.

Stanton tried to open his eyes, but only the left one would fully respond. The right eyelid went halfway up and stopped as the flesh above his eye filled with fluid. He realized he was on his back, looking up at a man standing above him with a metal pipe in hand. The man lifted it again and slammed it down onto Stanton's head. Then everything went black.

20

Alma Parr checked the clock. It was 7:23 pm, time to call it a day. He turned off his computer and rose, stretching the muscles in his neck and back. He glanced at the empty spot on top of a three-foot high pillar in the corner. One of Mike Tyson's signed boxing gloves was supposed to sit there, but Tyson left Vegas the day before Parr had enough free time to go down to the sporting goods store where he was signing autographs. He would come back. Celebrities past their prime had a natural affinity for this city. They always came back.

He said goodbye to the few people hanging around at that hour and found his Mustang parked in a handicapped spot out front. Parr flipped on his sunglasses as the engine roared to life, then he took off out of the parking lot.

The streets were busy, but he maneuvered expertly through the mass of SUVs, cabs, luxury cars, and family sedans. At a stoplight, he pulled his Browning out of the holster and placed it on the passenger seat. He drove well above eighty miles per hour as darkness blanketed the city and the artificial lights glittered like fallen stars. It was a twenty-minute drive to his house in Paradise Hills.

The road wound up the hill like a coiled snake and offered a view of the valley below and the lake that wasn't more than a couple of miles away. There was a country club nearby as well, with two lush golf courses. Parr had never set foot there. That would have gotten him in trouble. He had no patience for condescending people.

The road took him past what had once been a manmade forest, where developers had planted a variety of trees, but in 1981 a fire wiped out a good half of them. The burnt remains stood like skeletons along the side of the road. Parr thought they added beauty to the stretch of road. Everything in Paradise Hills was planned and built by man. The chaos and unpredictability of nature was pleasing, and it was where he felt most comfortable.

His home, white with a terracotta Spanish-tiled roof, was built on a plateau. The driveway was long and the house was far enough from the road that he couldn't hear the traffic. He parked near his garage and stepped out. The sky was lit with stars. They were never visible in the city, but out here he felt as if he were alone and that they sparkled just for him.

He went inside and threw his keys in a clay bowl decorated with Native American designs. The house was filled with bearskin rugs, hand-carved wooden art depicting wolves and deer, and a few hunting trophies. Massive antlers hung in the living room over a bookcase, and several holstered firearms dangled from them. He placed his Browning back in its holster and hung it up with the others.

At the counter of the bar that he had built near the kitchen, he took out a glass and put in two ice cubes before filling a third of the glass with amber liquid from a whiskey bottle waiting there. It was a special type of whiskey made in Tennessee: Heth's Tears Whiskey.

His grandfather had been a bootlegger there during Prohibition, and the company he had started had grown into a legitimate brewery and distillery. The business had been left to Parr and his three brothers. Parr's brothers ran the operation in Tennessee and sent him his share of the profits once a year in the form of a cashier's check. His brothers hadn't argued with him when he'd requested this arrangement. He was the oldest brother and, technically, the business was entirely his. His grandfather had bequeathed it all to him, believing that it was the right of the oldest to inherit and to distribute to the family as he saw fit.

There was a knock at the door. He finished the drink in two gulps and answered it. Outside stood a leggy brunette in a tight red dress and heels, smiling wryly. He stood aside and let her in. She threw her purse on the counter and began fixing herself a cocktail at the bar.

"You didn't call me today," she said.

"I was busy."

"With what?"

"Same old horseshit."

"You're such a poet."

He walked to the sliding glass door that overlooked the valley. A fire burned in the distance on the side of a hill. It gave the night a dim orange glow. "How was work?"

"Is that really what you want to talk about?"

"No. I just thought that's what normal people do. Talk about work."

She brought out two cocktails and handed him one. She placed one hand on his shoulder and took a sip of her drink with the other.

"I love this view. I can only see a brick wall from my apartment."

"What drink is this?"

"Mojito."

"Tastes like queer juice."

"You don't have to always be the macho swinging dick around me, Al. I don't care. I see through you just like you see through me." She pulled him toward her and placed her mouth over his, sliding her tongue past his lips.

He threw back the drink and tossed the glass on the floor.

Parr woke to a blanket of stars in an otherwise pitch-black sky. He was lying on his carpeted balcony. He sat up and glanced at his neighbors' homes to make sure none of them were up. The lights were on in two of the homes, but the blinds were drawn.

Karen lay next to him, nude except for his shirt which covered her torso like a blanket. He stood up and pulled on his boxers before going inside. He went to the bathroom and raised the toilet seat, staring at himself in the mirror and flexing his gargantuan triceps as he pissed.

When he was through, he washed his hands and brushed his teeth. Karen came in and slid past him, running her nails along his back. She slipped into the shower but picked up the towel first and placed it on the shower rod.

Parr froze, staring at the towel. His wife used to do the same thing because she could never reach the towel rack from the shower. The pain struck him like a blow to his chest. He spit out the foam in his mouth and rinsed as Karen told him about something that had happened earlier in the day. He walked out and went into the bedroom. On the nightstand was a photo that was nearly eight years old. *Has it really been that long?* He thought back, counting each year.

The photo of him and his wife, Terry, had been taken while they were climbing Mount Hood. Their faces were pressed together as she took the photo with a disposable camera at the summit. He picked up the photo and stared at it.

"You never talk about her."

Startled, he glanced up to see Karen standing there with a towel wrapped around her slender physique.

"Go finish your shower."

She stood there quietly a moment. "I'm here, Al. I have flesh and blood and feelings, and I have things to say. I have opinions. She doesn't anymore. She's not coming back, but I'm here. I'm *here*. And I can't compete with a dead woman."

"There's no competition," he said, staring up at her. "Get dressed and get the fuck out."

"You don't mean that."

He sighed and put the photo back. "No, I don't. You can stay if you like."

"What happened to her, Al?"

He leaned back on the headboard. "She was... she was at work.

It was an office building near the—"

The phone rang. He looked at it a moment, not entirely sure what it was. He could count on one hand the number of people who had his home phone number.

"Hello?" he said.

"Al, sorry to catch you at home. It's Mindi."

"How the hell did you get my home number?"

"Oh, sorry. I got it from the assistant chief. I thought it would be okay."

"What do you want? I'm tired."

"Um, you know that guy Orson's brought in from San Diego? Jon Stanton?"

"What about him?"

"He didn't come in to the precinct today."

"So what? Maybe he got laid."

"No, he's not like that. I'm worried. He's not picking up his phone and he's not at his hotel. This doesn't seem like something he would do."

"What've you known the guy for, a week? How the hell do you know what he would do?"

"Al, I'm asking you for help."

He ran his hand over his head. "I know. Look, he probably just got caught up in a casino or something. Maybe he got trashed and passed out somewhere. He's not just going to disappear. Have you called Orson?"

"Yeah, his phone is off."

"I'll tell you what—I'll check it out tomorrow. Ask around and see if anybody's seen him."

"Okay. I guess that's better than nothing. See ya tomorrow."

He hung up and placed the tip of the antennae in his mouth, biting down softly with his front teeth. He looked to see if Karen was still there, but she had gone back to the shower. He dialed a number.

"This is Danny."

"Hey, it's Alma. You on my mark?"

"Just got an update from the team an hour ago. They're on

him."

"Where?"

"House on Flower. He went inside earlier today and hasn't come out yet."

"How much earlier?"

"'Bout ten o'clock."

"He's been inside one house since ten and you didn't call me?"

Danny crunched on something and chewed. "I figured he had some girl there or something."

"Gimme the line to the van."

"I don't think I should do that, Al. It's against protocol."

"You shitting me? Gimme that fucking number, you little pissant, or I swear to all that's holy I'll be at your house in an hour to get it from you."

"Wow, that's an overreaction. Calm down, man. You're gonna get an ulcer or something."

"I'm not fucking around. Gimme the number."

Danny gave him the number and Parr grabbed a pen off the nightstand and wrote it down on his palm. "Thanks. And I was just kidding about kicking your ass."

Parr dialed. A male voice answered on the third ring. "Station Three."

"This is Captain Alma Parr. You folks are on my dime right now. I need an update."

"Looks good, Captain. He's just inside a house over here on Flower."

"What's your name?"

"Henry, sir."

"Henry, I want you to go knock on the door. If anyone answers, you apologize and say you got the wrong house and leave. But look inside and see if the mark's there."

"Gotchya. Hang on." There was some shuffling around then the sound of a door opening. There were footsteps on pavement, knocking, and then a long wait. "Don't look like anybody's home."

"Any lights on?"

"Nope."

"Go around back and see if you can look into any of the windows."

"'Kay, one sec… back window into the basement is broken out."

Parr bit down and shook his head. *The stupid bastard let him slip away.* "Get in the house and see if anyone's home."

"Um, we don't have a warrant or nothin'."

"I'll take the heat. Just get in there."

"All right. Lemme check the door… back door's open."

"Radio the van and tell your partner you need back up."

"All right. I gotta hang up, though."

"Call me right back. I'm not fucking around—you call me right back."

"I will, sir."

Parr hung up and paced the room. The Homeland Security Unit at the Metro PD had been created in response to 9/11, and it had been stacked with college grads looking to get some experience before moving up to the feds to start careers as bureaucrats. A few were solid cops, but Parr hadn't interacted much with them. He should have stuck to uniforms he knew.

His phone rang. "Yeah, this is Parr."

"Henry again, sir. We're inside the house."

Parr heard Henry's partner shout, "Clear."

"Upstairs is clear, sir. We're heading down."

"Stay on your toes."

Parr bit his thumbnail and walked to the bar in the living room. He pinned the phone to his shoulder with his cheek and poured himself more whiskey. He went to his balcony and stood watching the fire as helicopters dropped hundreds of gallons of water over it.

There was shouting then swearing coming from the phone.

"Uh oh," Henry said.

"What? What's wrong?"

"We're gonna have to call it in, sir. We got a body here."

21

Bill James got out of the shower and looked over his body in the full-length mirror. The years had been good to him, mostly free of the hard labor that he'd seen age others. He had no idea why society put such value on hard work. It aged people, caused them pain, and wore out their bodies and minds. It was for suckers. If they wanted to get rich, people had to work intelligently and with calculated forethought towards the future. Nothing else would get them rich.

He went to his walk-in closet and chose the Polo suit with the white pinstripes. Hand-made Italian sandals went over his sockless feet and he chose a black t-shirt with no tie. Once he was dressed, he looked himself over and knew what was missing. He had been stalling, hoping he wouldn't have to add it, but that would be a decision based solely on principle instead of practicality. Since he was a teenager, he'd sworn never to make decisions based only on principle.

He finally relented, reached into a drawer on his massive mahogany dresser, and pulled out a snub-nose revolver, which he tucked into his belt at the small of his back. He hadn't carried a gun for forty years. The thought of it filled him with dread. People who carried guns naturally ended up in situations in which they had to use them. The universe wasn't stupid. It gave back exactly what he put into it. But he feared the alternative might have been worse.

He left his suite and took the elevator down to the casino floor. He passed most of the tables, heading to one where a crowd had gathered. A chain-smoking Asian man sat at a black-jack table, a massive stack of chips piled in front of him. His glasses were down on the brim of his nose, and he was dispassionately analyzing the cards in his hand. He hit at sixteen and pulled a four. The dealer busted at twenty-three. The crowd cheered as the dealer counted out his bet: six thousand on one hand.

The pit boss came up to James and stood next to him quietly, like a soldier awaiting orders. Hot streaks required the commander's attention.

"How long has he been winning?" James asked.

"Just over twelve hours."

James smirked. The house had a nearly two percent edge over an amateur blackjack player, which meant that for every dollar played, the casino kept two cents as profit and paid the remaining ninety-eight cents back out to the player. Bet after bet, the edge would grind away at the player's money, eventually taking all of it. In the long run no one could beat the edge. The casino could be beaten in short bursts, usually no more than an hour or so if someone was really on a hot streak. Few players had the self-control to make big bets a small number of times then walk away while they were ahead. In forty years of working in casinos, James had seen few people who could do it. Gambler's avarice was uncontrollable, and they were unable to pull themselves away from tables even if they were millions of dollars ahead.

Twelve hours of winning was statistically impossible. James studied a couple of the man's bets and his hands. He walked up behind the man, who was reaching to throw his cards to the dealer, and grabbed his wrist. Twisting it, he exposed several thousand-dollar chips the man had palmed.

It was an old trick that had worked well before cameras were above every table. The player would place one or even two thousand-dollar chips under a stack of hundreds as his bet. If he leaned the stack toward the dealer at just the right angle, the entire stack appeared to be hundreds. If he won, he showed the dealer the thousand-dollar chips and claimed his prize. If he lost, he threw down his cards and on the way out, he would pick up the chips at the bottom of the stack. Glue could be applied to the fingers to make it easier, but the experts could pull out the bottom chips without making the stack fall.

Two security personnel rushed over and grabbed the Asian man. They lifted him out of his seat and dragged him toward the interrogation room at the back of the casino. James watched him go. He wanted to be back there with his own brass knuckles, but that wasn't the way things were handled anymore. Nowadays the police were called, the man would be cited, and lawyers would battle it out in court for a few months. He thought that even the cheats might have preferred a single, clean beating so they could move on with their lives.

James turned to the pit boss. "Fire the dealer now. Have him escorted out. Fire whoever was manning the eye in the sky for this table. Same thing, escort them out. That's really important. If they're in on it, they may be keeping a stack of chips somewhere in the building."

"Will do. Anything else?"

"Follow up with me tomorrow," James said before walking away. He knew the pit boss would be nervous that he was under suspicion as well, and would work hard to clean up the mess. But after the pit boss had carried out his orders, James would fire him, too.

James made his way over to the high rollers' lounge, where men in suits and tuxedos were gathered around several tables. The gorgeous women on their arms could've been ripped out of the pages of any glamorous magazine. He looked for the blackjack table in the corner with the black dealer, a woman who used to be in his shows. He had found that her beauty and charm kept the high rollers, most of whom were old white men, drinking and gambling.

"Hey, Suzan," he said as he sat down.

"Mr. James. Hope you're having a pleasant evening."

"Good enough."

"Would you like to play a hand?"

"No, thank you. I'm waiting for someone."

He watched her deal to the other two gentlemen at the table. They made moderately large bets, three or four thousand a hand, but their minds were on the women, whom James had planted in the high roller rooms of other casinos. The women would get to know the men, get them drinking, and then suggest they go to the Havana because they preferred the atmosphere there. As soon as the men ran out of money, the women excused themselves to the restroom and never returned to the table.

Cal Robertson sat down and James glanced over at him. James had known many powerful men who had aged and watched their power fade. They wanted to feel relevant, as if they still mattered, and often they were stubborn just because they wanted the attention.

"How long have we known each other, Cal? Thirty years?"

"Yeah," he said, laying out a credit card that the dealer swiped. "Twenty thousand in chips, please."

"This deal has to go through."

"You're betting on something that's not going to happen, Bill. Cuba will never allow gambling again. They have bad memories. The mob ran everything down there when all of that was going on. People were starving in the streets, and the casino owners were moving millions of dollars out of the country every day. Even as bad as they got it now, they're not going back to that."

"I disagree. I go down there a lot, Cal. People are sick of the government telling them what career they're going to have and who they can or can't talk to. They realize communism was a mistake. Even the damned Commies know that but they can't just come out and say, 'Hey, by the way, sorry for the mass murders. Turns out communism doesn't work.' They'd be crucified afterwards. They're going to do it in degrees. But the casinos are coming, and we need to stake our claim now."

Cal bet five thousand on a hand and pushed with the dealer. He swore under his breath and bet another five on the next hand.

"Do you know how many grandchildren I have? Twenty-four, with two more on the way. I've got a legacy. I want to leave them something. If this merger goes through, and we can't acquire it 'cause the Reds won't allow it, we'll lose our shirts. Do you hear me on that, Bill? We will lose this casino. The banks will tear it apart piece by piece and sell it like a junk car. Why take the risk?"

"Risk is how you get rich. You wanna be remembered as owning a two-bit casino that's going to be taken over by pussy Harvard MBAs after we're gone? That's not where we come from, Cal. We're bigger than that. What if Cuba does pay off? We won't be multi-millionaires, Cal. We'll be billionaires. You can give each of your grandkids ten million dollars and not even miss it. We can influence things. I got no delusions. I know I'm on the way out of this life. I got, what, ten good years left, if I'm lucky? I can't spend the money in that time, but I can change things. I can influence the way things work. I can set up think tanks and foundations. I can really change things."

Cal bet his last ten thousand on a single hand and hit twenty-one. "You heard that saying, I think it was Churchill who said it, 'If you're not a liberal by twenty you got no heart, but if you're not conservative by thirty you've got no brains.'? I'm fine with things the way they are. I'm not looking to shake things up. I'm sorry, Bill. My answer's no."

James looked down at the floor at a scrap of trash, a paper from a marker. He picked it up and placed it in the garbage can underneath the table on the dealer's side. "Then we got nothing else to discuss."

James returned to his suite, where he walked out on the balcony and looked over the city. His city. No, that wasn't true anymore. It had belonged to him and those like him maybe three or four decades ago. But Las Vegas was excitement and immorality, and it was the purview of the young to stake a claim on those things.

He let the breeze blow over his face for a while then took out his cell phone and dialed a number.

"This is Bill," he told the person on the other end. He hesitated a moment. "The old man won't play ball. Get him out of the game."

He hung up quickly, as if that would absolve him, then set the phone down on a glass table near him.

Lord forgive me.

22

Alma Parr's Mustang screeched to a stop outside the home with the police tape across the front door.

He got out of the car, made his way past three cruisers, and ducked underneath the police tape to get into the house. He glanced back once to see if anybody was watching. He saw only a handful of people out on their patios. The house was filled with uniforms. Some were actually working, but most were chatting, laughing, and talking about unrelated things. They made him sick.

He walked into a crowd of six or so officers and barked, "Get to work or get outta this house."

They dispersed, and he found the stairs leading to the basement. The atmosphere was much calmer downstairs, where forensic techs were already dusting for latent prints. One of the techs, whom Parr knew as a fiber expert, was on his hands and knees brushing through the carpet with a little comb. When he found something of interest, he pulled out a little plastic baggie, placed his specimen inside, and went back to brushing.

There was also someone else Parr didn't recognize; he had no uniform or badge.

"Can I help you?" Parr asked him.

"Oh, hi. I'm Preston Holbrook from the *Sun*."

"Well, Preston Holbrook from the *Sun*, you're in my fucking crime scene." He looked around. "Who let a reporter into my crime scene?" he shouted.

The room went quiet. No one dared to speak or look around.

Everyone pretended to be busy. Parr turned back to Holbrook.

"I know you parasites got people inside my department. They give you the hot tips, and you get 'em some cash or hookers or basketball tickets. You corrupt good men just trying to get by. Am I right?" he said with a smile.

The reporter, seemingly uncertain if Parr was joking or serious, just smiled awkwardly. "Um, I wouldn't know anything about that."

Parr placed his hand on the back of Holbrook's neck, the smile still on his face. He squeezed tightly and pulled him near. "You're gonna tell me who your source was."

"You're kidding, right? There's no way I'm saying anything. And get your fucking hands off me, or you'll be getting a call from my lawyer."

Smiling, Parr nodded and slammed his elbow into Holbrook's face. The reporter flew off his feet and onto his back. "You guys see him assault me?" Parr said. "I think he's drunk. Better take him to the tank and let him sleep it off. Don't let him out until I come see him tomorrow."

A couple of the uniforms glanced at each other, helped Holbrook to his feet, and led him up the stairs.

"He's over here, Captain."

Parr turned towards the voice and spotted Javier and Jay. They were standing off to the side in a bedroom. The room was empty except for a large chest, a bed, and a dresser. Parr walked in and stood in front of the chest.

"We didn't want to bag him until you got here."

Parr slipped on latex gloves. One of the forensic techs in the room was about to say something but caught himself. Parr glanced at him. He averted his gaze and walked out of the room. The nerds bugged Parr. They weren't cops, and they never had to deal with victims or the late-night hospital and morgue visits, but ever since that damned TV show they acted as if they ran the police force.

Parr lifted the lid of the chest. Inside, a body was curled into a ball. The wound on the back of the man's head looked like a gunshot wound, but there was too much hair in the way to see for sure. Parr knew who it was and didn't have to check, but he did anyway. He tilted the head to get a clear look. It was Marty Scheffield.

"What happened?" he said to no one in particular.

"We don't know," Javier replied. "The assistant from the ME's office thinks he's been dead for two days but only recently stuffed in there. They're not sure yet. They gotta do the autopsy."

"Why would anybody do this to him? He had no enemies. He never hurt nobody."

Jay said, "I know. I'm sorry. I know you liked him."

Parr gazed off into space for a few moments then said, "Did we find Stanton?"

"No, but a neighbor in the back reported seeing two men earlier in the day. One wearing a ski mask and the other chasing after him. Description of the pursuer matches Stanton."

"And the neighbor didn't call it in?"

"No. They said they didn't want to get involved."

"Oh, they're involved now. Get their asses to the station. If they resist tell them they're suspects and it's better they cooperate. Arrest 'em if they still cause a fuss."

"I'm on it."

"And, Jay, better cancel that trip to San Diego. I need you here."

"You got it."

Parr turned back to the chest. He had known Marty more than a decade. Marty had helped bring him onto the force. He'd been Parr's sergeant when he'd first started. Marty had come to his house when his wife left him, since he had nowhere else to go. Parr had helped Marty relearn how to read and write after his accident.

Parr decided he wasn't giving the killer the chance to get away with it. If Jon Stanton was in any way responsible for this, he would not be leaving Las Vegas alive.

23

Stanton stood on the edge of the platform at the front of the church as music started to play. It was Bach, but it was distant and muffled. He hardly heard it because his stomach was so wound up in knots that he had a massive headache. His best man, a friend from long ago, was standing next to him. Melissa stepped out into the aisle and walked toward him and his tears began to flow. He'd thought they would be together until the end. He had pictured college graduations, weddings, retirements, old age… he'd never thought he would be saying good-bye to her at thirty-four and having to speak to her lovers.

Pain had a taste. It had a presence. It was a thing. If allowed, pain could dig into a person like a worm and spread through the whole body. Pain affected not only the body but the soul, too. The dreary-eyed who drove to jobs they hated and returned home to families they despised may as well have been riding in their own coffins.

Pain was what woke him—the thought of his children raised by another man while their memories of him faded until he was an abstraction in their minds. He was their father, yes, but more just the form of a father. He pictured Melissa standing on the stage, but he wasn't the one next to her.

Stanton woke on his back. Above him was concrete. A light-bulb with a long cord dangled from the center of the ceiling. The floors were bare cement, but there was no dirt or dust. The walls were also clean. He could see a furnace and an intricate array of pipes and wires, and shelves or cupboards filled the other side of the room.

His head pounded. It came in circular waves that started at the back and the circles grew tighter and tighter until they were focused in the space between his eyes. The pain radiated through him so forcefully that he gagged, turning to the side as vomit spewed out of his mouth.

When he was through vomiting, he lay flat on his back, the room spinning around him, and he tried to monitor his breathing. He took long, deep breaths and exhaled slowly, focusing his mental energy on the spot just two inches below his navel. He pictured flowing water running through his arms, legs, torso and head. He let the water pool at his navel and slowly spread to his limbs, his lungs, and his heart, returning strength to them.

Stanton visualized this for a long time before he felt well enough to sit up. He noticed for the first time that thick plastic cuffs wrapped each of his wrists, which were behind his back, held together by plastic bars. A rope was around his ankles but it was loose and moved freely.

The pounding in his head returned and he had to close his eyes. He sent the water from his navel to the back of his head. He pictured that the pain was a fire, a raging inferno in the space in his head. The water cooled it, brought it under control so he could function, or at least stop focusing entirely on the pain.

His wrists were bound so tightly that he was certain they were turning a light purple by now. He slid his arms under his legs and brought his hands in front of him. The more he fought the intricate cuffs the tighter they became. He put his foot in between his wrists and pushed as hard as he could, but the cuffs didn't budge.

Stanton ran his eyes over the windowless walls. A small set of wooden stairs led up to a door that was bolted with several impressive-looking locks. Farther down the room was a metal cabinet. Its doors were open a few inches but he couldn't see inside. There was also a poster of a nude woman at the beach, her toes dug into the sand. Her youthful glow came through in a massive smile as she lifted one free hand in an apathetic but sexual gesture.

Stanton's gaze went back to the cabinet. It was out of the ordinary, the statistical outlier, the thing that didn't belong.

He reached down and began to loosen the ropes around his ankles so he could make it to the cabinet, then heard a phone ringing upstairs. He held his breath, listening intently. It rang five times and stopped. As he reached back down to the rope, he heard another sound: footsteps heading toward the basement door.

25

Parr walked into the precinct at six in the morning. He hadn't slept. He didn't need to. In Fallujah, he had been dropped into enemy territory with a shortage of rations. His pack had to weigh less than twenty-five pounds to keep him light. Ammunition, the radio, his rifle, a handgun and a knife made up over fifteen pounds. That left little allowance for food and water, so he was expected to find these on his own. A small container in the bottom right pocket of his pack held prescription amphetamines given to him by the army medic. Taking amphetamines was voluntary for the snipers, and many refused. But a few, the ones the army didn't expect to come back, got the script.

He slept in one-hour bursts whenever he could. Usually, he would find a car parked in a driveway and sneak under it or find an underpass or an alley. Once, he'd slept in a large trash container. He'd been up for three days, and he'd known he would be out for a while as soon as he fell asleep. The trash was the nearest place he could find that didn't involve an intensive search.

Sometime after dusk, voices woke him then he heard an argument and gunfire. The bin was too tight to pull out his rifle, so he took out his pistol and held it close to him as he lifted the lid. Three people in civilian clothes were on the ground, where a thick black liquid mixed with the dirt to form mud. The two men standing over them with assault rifles exchanged a few words before going through the victims' pockets. Roving bandits were common in the country then. Ex-soldiers and Saddam's Republican Guard found it lucrative to scour the smaller towns and villages, raping and robbing along the way.

Screams came from the house. Parr looked over and saw a woman in her forties, hysterical from the sight of her family shot to death on her driveway. She ran to them and one of the soldiers grabbed her. They laughed as they dragged her back inside.

There were six targets in the area and Parr's mission was clear: strike as many of them as he could and get out. The incident he'd woken up to was not his fight. He sat in the trashcan, surrounded by garbage, and thought about sneaking out and moving on. He tapped his pistol on his forehead. This war was going to take his life but he would be damned if it took his soul, too.

Parr snuck out of the trash bin and stayed low as he ran to the front door of the house. The door was unlocked. He could hear the woman screaming from there and he went inside. The house smelled like jasmine. Decorations cluttered the walls and hand-made rugs covered the floors. It was a modern-looking home. If he had seen it under different circumstances it would not have looked out of place in any American city.

He followed the screams, which led him around the kitchen to a back bedroom. He peered in and saw the men pinning the woman down. Parr tucked his pistol away and pulled out his fourteen-inch Heavy Bowie. He held the serrated blade facing down as he slipped into the room.

One man was on top of her and the other was holding her arms down. Parr was in a duck walk, his knees almost touching the carpet as he came up to the bed. He stood and lifted the rapist's head. He inserted the tip of the blade between his neck and shoulder, severing the voice box to prevent him from screaming. Parr twisted the knife so violently that a ragged chunk of flesh flew off his neck and onto the woman.

The other man was nude from the waist down as well and had left his weapon on the nightstand. He leapt for it as Parr jumped onto the bed, stepped over the woman, and swung the knife down with both hands, throwing his weight behind it. It smashed into the man's spine, breaking it instantly. The man collapsed like a heap of Jell-O. Parr could see consciousness in his eyes. He was paralyzed, not dead. Parr looked up at the woman and said in his broken Arabic, "Let the bastard starve to death." He left without looking back.

As he walked down the hall of the precinct, he wondered what had happened to that woman.

"Al," Mindi said, running up behind him. "Any word on Jon?"

"Nothing yet. We got one of Marty's neighbors here and I'm gonna find out what he saw."

"Oh, right. I'm sorry about Marty."

"It is what it is."

"If you need anything, like, I dunno—"

"I'm fine." He turned down another corridor and headed to the interrogation room.

Mindi had to quicken her pace to keep up. "Do you want me to come with you?"

"No."

"I could help."

"If you want to help get on the horn to some people in San Diego and dig up some dirt about Stanton."

"I really don't think he had anything to do with this."

Parr stopped and turned to her. "You remember that body we found? The crispy critter in the car?"

"Yeah."

"Some of the cholos told me that was Stanton's work."

"No way. I don't believe it."

"Yeah? Well you tell me how some piece of shit thug on the streets of Vegas knows Jon Stanton's name."

"It couldn't be him."

"Why? 'Cause you think he's such a great guy? Lemme tell you somethin', Mindi—you trust nobody. Everybody in this world is capable of anything. It's just a matter of price. Even your mom would do anything for the right price."

"My mother's a bitch. Of course she would do it."

"I ain't playin' around here. You said you wanted to help, so help. Get on that phone and tell me what kinda guy we're dealing with." Parr turned around and didn't wait for her. He went through a large gray door into the interrogation rooms.

Behind a two-way mirror, an older man with a white beard sat thumbing through his phone. Parr watched him a second. He appeared to be nervous; he glanced around and swore under his breath every few seconds. Parr reached up and pulled out the cord connecting the video recorder to the camera before stepping into the room.

He shut the door behind him and sat down across from the man.

"Are you a cop?"

"Yes," Parr said.

"'Bout fucking time. I been sitting on my ass for two hours."

"That's a shame," Parr said, leaning back in the chair.

"It is a shame, and I've had just about enough of it. I want out of here right now."

"Sorry, can't do that just yet."

"Well, then, I want to speak to your supervisor."

"My supervisor ain't here. He's telling the parents of Marty Scheffield that their boy's dead."

They sat quietly for a few moments.

"Marty's dead? Nobody told me. How'd he die?"

"He was taken out. Got the call a few minutes ago from the medical examiner. One gunshot wound to the cerebellum. Real professional. He never felt a thing."

"Wow. Well, look, I'm sorry about Marty. I liked the kid. He always mowed my lawn when he was out mowing his."

"That's sweet of him." Parr ran his fingers around the table edge.

"So do you need me to identify his body or something?"

"No, his sister did that already."

"Then what do you need from me?"

"You know, if you would've had some balls and called this in when it happened, maybe we woulda caught the son of a bitch who did this."

"There's no law against that. I don't have to call anything in if I don't want to. And how the hell was I supposed to know what this was? I just saw one guy chasing another guy. They jumped over my fence into the street and were gone."

Parr took out his phone and brought up a picture of the actor Edward Norton. "This the guy you saw chasing the other guy?"

"Yup, that's him."

"You sure?"

"Of course I'm sure."

"No uncertainty at all? This is the guy. You're positive?"

"Well, not a hundred percent, but yeah, I think that's him."

Parr put his phone away. "You didn't see shit, did you?"

"It only lasted two, maybe three seconds. But that's the guy."

"And the other guy was in a ski mask you said?"

"Yeah. He was a bigger guy. Tall. He tried my backdoor and then hopped my fence. I never saw nothing of him."

"Where'd they go after they hopped your fence?"

"Out into the street. They ran up for maybe half a block and then I couldn't see them anymore."

"Did you see anybody in Marty's house the past few days? Think carefully before you answer. I'm not saying chicks in bikinis. I'm saying anybody. Who did you see there?"

"I can't think of a single person other than the meter reader."

"Meter reader?"

"Yeah. Someone from the electric company. They came and read his meters in the backyard."

"When?"

"Two days ago maybe."

"Did you talk to them?"

"No I was in the shower. Just looked over and saw him reading the meters."

Parr folded his beefy arms. "And this was someone from NV Energy?"

"Um, yeah. Yeah, I think that's what the uniform said. Yeah."

"Did you see what he drove up to Marty's house in?"

"No, I only saw him in the backyard."

Parr leaned forward and stared into the man's eyes. "Next time you see someone who needs help, you fucking help them."

The man didn't respond. Parr left the room. He went and hooked the camera back up before he pulled out his phone and Googled NV Energy.

26

Stanton hid the slack of the rope underneath his legs. He leaned his head back against the wall to make himself appear weak. The footsteps descended and he heard a key insert into the lock and twist. Then the door opened.

The man was dressed in jeans and a green jacket. A ski mask covered his face. He was wearing gloves and thick boots. His neck was covered. Stanton knew instantly that this man wasn't an amateur. He had hidden everything that could've indicated his ethnicity. The only thing he couldn't cover were his eyes, which were dark brown.

The abductor stood in front of Stanton, staring at him. He reached into his jacket and pulled out a large hunting knife, the type used to gut a deer. Stanton's heart raced but he was practiced at hiding his reactions. The abductor paced slowly around the room, his hands behind him. He was tapping the knife gently against a watch, making a metallic clink. His head was down as he paced.

Stanton could see the hesitation in his body language. The nervous tapping, the pacing... he had come down there certain of his choice, but seeing Stanton had changed something. The future was no longer definite. Stanton knew he had only a few moments before the man made up his mind again.

"I was being followed," Stanton said. The clinking stopped and the abductor turned to him. "There was a white van. It was in a classic tailing pattern called the Three-Hook Pattern. There are three cars, one far enough away from the mark that he can still see him without the mark noticing. Then you have a second car behind the first, far away but close enough to see him. Then you have a third car trailing the other two. The mark can only see the first car, so you switch which car is the first car at regular intervals. They were in a five-minute pattern with me. White van, brown Chrysler, and a black SUV. The Three-Hook is usually used by law enforcement. They were tailing me."

Stanton saw the man's chest heaving just a bit more. He was either nervous or building up courage.

"They'll find me here, eventually. Dead cop will bring the entire force down on this case. Maybe they'll bring in the feds, too. If I'm alive, it'll be a kidnapping case. It won't even go to Robbery-Homicide, where the top detectives are. If you're playing the numbers, you have the highest probability of getting away with it if I'm alive."

The abductor didn't move, then the knife came out again. He held it up near his face and ran his finger along the edge before he spun around and walked back through the open door. As he heard the door lock, Stanton exhaled loudly. He began to loosen the ropes around his ankles, then he lifted himself onto his hands and into an upright squat. His hands were still bound, but his feet were free.

The cabinet was about twenty feet away. He made his way over to the cabinet and stuck his finger between the doors, opening them only a few centimeters at a time to ensure they wouldn't creak.

On the bottom shelf he found coiled cable wire, a pair of pliers and work gloves. The middle shelves were empty and the top shelves held screws, nails, a glue gun and a few other tools. He took the pliers and spun them around so they were facing downward. The cuffs had a little hinge that held the locks in place. He tried putting the pliers' teeth around the hinge to snap it, but he couldn't get a good grip. Instead, he sat down and pulled his wrists under his legs, bringing his hands to the front. He pushed with his legs against his hands, gripping the hinge with the pliers.

The hinge on the cuffs snapped and he gently placed them on the floor. He put the pliers back and walked up the stairs to the door. The lock was a simple doorknob. This wasn't a dungeon or part of a premeditated plan. This was a basement, and he'd been brought here on a whim.

Stanton went back to the cabinet and sifted through the nails. He found one that was long and slim like a paperclip. He took it back to the door at the top of the stairs and placed his ear on the frame. The other side was quiet. He didn't hear footsteps or voices. Gently, he placed the tip of the nail into the lock and pushed.

A little at a time, the nail went in until it hit the metal cylinder and the lock button. There was a click as it unlocked. Stanton didn't open it right away. He looked around the basement for a weapon. He went back to the cabinet, took a six-inch Phillips head screwdriver, and held it against his wrist, concealing it. He went back to the door and opened it.

Roughly twelve more stairs led up to the second floor. He slipped off his shoes and climbed each one as lightly as possible, his eyes fixed above him. If the abductor returned with a gun, Stanton would be an immobile target on a downhill slope. He would be dead.

The edges of the stairs nearest the wall were the least likely locations to develop creaks, and he placed his feet there. He was halfway up the stairs when he heard a door slam. His heart jumped into his throat and he gripped the screwdriver tighter. He could climb the rest of the stairs in maybe three seconds. If he surprised the man, even a little, Stanton might make it up there.

A car roared to life as a garage door opened. The engine noise faded then disappeared as the garage door closed again. Stanton quickly climbed the rest of the stairs. Without searching the home, he just looked for the nearest exit—the front door. He hurried over and unlocked it, glancing back once as he walked out into the darkness of the night.

27

Chief of Police Tom Brandish Keele walked from his Chevy Tahoe to the precinct doors and looked the building up and down. It looked so damned... modern. Everything was modernized. His detectives carried iPads, took notes with rubber styluses and dictated into digital recorders. When he'd first started on the force as a young buck of eighteen, nearly forty years ago, Las Vegas was nothing more than a few hotels and horrible restaurants owned by the New York mob. Those days detectives wrote everything in a little notepad, but most of the time they didn't have to; they were expected to memorize every single detail about every single case. Sure, they wrote it down at the end of the week in status reports, but that was it. And the status reports went up to bosses who didn't really look them over because the department trusted that what needed to be done was getting done. There was no IAD, no staff of attorneys to cover their asses, no complaints about brutality. Unless someone was shot or beaten severely enough to spend the night in a hospital claims of police brutality were unheard of.

At sixty-seven, looking at the building, Keele wondered if he should take his kids' advice and finally retire. Elected officials had no mandatory retirement age and he could realistically serve until he was dead or incapacitated. His kids were entrenched in their family life. They had baseball games, barbeques, school plays and dances. They had Sunday dinners and family vacations. For the past two years—since his wife had died of complications with pneumonia—all Keele had was an empty condo and a lifetime of memories. They were not enough to warm the other side of the bed at night.

He went into the building and nodded hello to the person at the front desk. When he was a new chief nineteen years ago he was attacked with memos, signature requests, overtime slips and interview requests the moment he stepped foot into any precinct. But now he had insulated himself well. He had four assistant chiefs who handled most of the work he used to do himself. Over them was an under-deputy who saw to the day-to-day business. He also had heads of staff for finance, general counsel, administrative staff, and intergovernmental relations. He delegated most of his work so that he could keep his eye on the big picture: cutting bureaucracy so that cops could focus on actually solving crimes. Striking that balance was tough, considering he had added more bureaucrats to the payroll than any chief in the city's history.

The elevator was about to take him up to his office when a hand parted them. Orson Hall stepped on, a coffee in his hand. He faced forward, waiting for the doors to close.

"I need to talk to you," Keele said.

"'Bout what?"

"Daniel Steed's case and that detective you flew in."

"I can't believe it myself. I keep hoping he shacked up with some hooker and just has his phone off, but the assistant I assigned to him says he's been incommunicado for an entire day. I'm not quite in panic mode, but I think that we should—"

"They found him."

"What?"

"They found him. Jon Stanton, right? They found him. He called the emergency line from a gas station."

"Why wasn't I told about this?"

"Take your dick out of that filly you got on the side and turn your damn phone on sometimes."

Orson took out his cell phone. It was off. "Oh. Didn't realize I did that. Where is he now?"

"He's here."

"I need to talk to him."

The elevator dinged and they stepped off. They said nothing else until they were behind the closed doors of Keele's plush corner office. Keele pulled a glass bottle out of a drawer and poured brandy. He offered some to Orson, who turned it down.

"You can't talk to him yet," Keele said. "I gave him to Alma."

"For what?"

"He seems to think your boy is involved in that homicide from a while back, the burn victim. He asked if he could have an hour with him alone before anyone else and I said it was okay."

"Tom, he's a friend a mine, out here as a favor to me."

"I didn't authorize pullin' off his fingernails or anything. He's just gonna talk to him."

"Yeah, 'cause that's all Alma does, right?"

"He's got some fire in him. That's for sure," Keele said, sitting in his chair with a grunt, his knees creaking. "But I trust the tough bastard more than I trust anyone here. Even you."

"Thanks, Tom. I appreciate that."

"Oh quit bein' so sensitive. Your friend's gonna be just fine and as soon as Alma's done with him you can go down there." He took a long drink and swirled the liquid in the glass. "I wanted to ask you if you think he could actually do something like that."

"Murder somebody? Jon Stanton? No way."

"How do you know?"

"I know him well enough to know he's not a killer."

"That's not what his file says."

"You looked up his file?"

Keele shrugged and took another drink. "Made a call to the chief over in San Diego. His file says he's had eight shootings in the line of duty. Seven were cleared as clean shootings, but they ain't sure about this last one."

"Every cop gets in that situation. Hell, how many shootings did you have? Ten? Twenty?"

"I've been at this three times as long and I came up in the days when bank robberies ended in gun battles. Different times."

"I can't picture him doing anything like that."

He finished the brandy and set the glass on the desk. "My old man was a philanderer. Slept with anything that moved. I didn't want to believe it and neither did my mama. We ignored it as much as we could. Then he gave my mama syphilis. She died'a that. She was too proud to go to a doctor, so it ate away at her mind. Damn thing lays dormant so long you don't even know you have it until it turns your brain to Swiss cheese. That's the trick, Orson. You gotta face that everyone is capable of everything."

Orson took a deep breath. "What you wanna do?"

"Nothing yet. All we got is rumors from some wetback dope dealers. I don't wanna move on a good cop if that's it. Give Alma a chance to play this out. If there's anything there, he'll find it."

28

It took Parr nearly half an hour to get through to someone at NV Energy who could answer his questions. He spoke with a manager named Nate who had a Texas twang. Parr gave him the address and asked who had been out to read the meters in the past three days.

"Sir, we barely do that anymore. It's only on some of them older homes. Usually we can just read 'em right here on our computers."

Parr thanked him for his time and hung up. The next step was to re-canvas the neighborhood. Uniforms had already canvassed two blocks in every direction but they hadn't asked about someone claiming to be from the electric company. Parr would have to grab some men and do it again. He looked at his watch and realized it was noon—most of the neighbors would be at work. He would have to wait until five or six and pull overtime. Besides, he had something much more important to do.

He had been purposely stalling and now forty-five minutes had passed. That was enough time for Stanton's nervous anticipation to cook a little in the interrogation room. Parr picked up his notepad, a pen and a photo of the unidentified body that had been nearly incinerated in a '97 Ford Taurus. He walked down the hall to the interrogation room where Stanton was waiting.

Jon Stanton didn't look like much. He was slender with a boyish face. He looked like the kind of guy who would stop to help someone on the side of the road, the type who celebrated every holiday and never had anything to complain about. Parr thought he looked like a missionary who was just a little too old to still be out there trying to convert people.

He sat down across from Stanton and looked him in the eyes. He took Stanton's wrists softly in his hands and looked at the deep purple bruising that wrapped around them.

"You sure you don't want a medic?" Parr asked.

"No," Stanton replied. "I'm fine, thanks."

"We didn't get a proper introduction earlier," Parr said, flashing his best smile. "I'm Alma Parr. I'm the captain over Robbery-Homicide."

"Alma. Do you know that's the name of a prophet in the *Book of Mormon*? He was a warrior. He left his people to wander through the wilderness and convert his enemies."

"Yeah, well, it's also an old German name and my grandparents were fresh-off-the-boat." Parr dropped his pen down on the pad. "I know you went through the story and what happened with the detective from Missing Persons 'bout an hour ago. That was just a formality. He needed that interview to close your case."

"I didn't know one had been opened."

"Mindi pulled some strings and had it opened. We usually wait seventy-two hours. Anyway, I was outside the mirror watching. So you picked the lock with a nail?"

"It's easy to do. Hairpins and paperclips actually work better but you use what you have."

Parr shook his head. "Quick on your feet. I like that."

"You must have been the same to get out of Iraq without a scratch."

Parr glared at him. "How'd you know I was in Iraq?"

"Oh, sorry. The tattoo."

Parr looked down at his biceps. Part of a tattoo of a rifle half-buried in the ground, a helmet propped on it and boots set in front, poked out from under his sleeve.

Stanton said, "The tattoo's really dark so I guessed it was pretty recent."

Parr shifted in his seat. "Yeah."

"Where were you?"

"Fallujah. For two tours." He cleared his throat. "I'd like to talk about you, Jon. I checked out your record. You cleared more cases than any other detective in Homicide over there in San Diego. That's pretty impressive. How do you do it?"

"Same as everyone else."

"That's not true. There was a note in the file—and excuse me for looking at this—but there was a note from the precinct shrink after you took out some dirtbag saying that you had a photographic memory and—what was the term he used? Unhealthy? Yeah, he said you had an *unhealthy* amount of empathy. That you can slip into other people's shoes and sometimes you can't stop yourself."

"I follow the same procedures every detective in every city does. I've gotten lucky a few times."

Parr looked down at the burn scar on his neck. "And you've gotten unlucky a few times, too, haven't you?"

Stanton sat quietly for a few moments then said, "Did you get divorced because of the war? Excuse me for looking, but I can see a slight indentation on your ring finger. You still wear the ring at night when no one's around, don't you?"

Parr gritted his teeth a moment, then said, "I want to know what happened to you when you were abducted."

"If you were standing behind the mirror, you already know. This is about something else and you don't want me to know what. Just be straight with me. It'll save us both time."

Parr exhaled loudly. His rhythm felt out of sync and frustration grew in his belly. The mention of the ring had thrown him off. He would have to stop wearing it while he slept.

He took the photo out from under the notepad and laid it in front of Stanton. It was a body that had been cooked to the driver's seat of a car. The figure was absolutely unidentifiable and his toothless mouth was agape, the gums charred black.

"What about it?" Stanton asked.

"Do you know anything about it?"

"No. When did it happen?"

"Four days before you flew into Vegas."

"If it happened before I got here, how am I supposed to know about it?"

"You tell me."

Stanton leaned back in the chair. "I'm guessing you're the one who put the tail on me."

"Jon, I'm gonna be straight with you, like you said. I don't give a rat's ass about this piece'a shit. He was probably some dope-head, pedophile, or who the shit knows what. But I do care about Marty Scheffield. I'm sure you wouldn't do that to another cop so you're not a suspect. You don't need to worry about that. But this crispy critter here I don't care about. You tell me you did it, and I say, 'Good.' I need to close this case and make sure it had nothing to do with Marty. You can clear that up for me right now."

"I'm not a dope fiend off the street thinking you're my friend, Alma. I can see the hatred in your eyes when you look at me. Your smile can't hide it."

Parr chuckled. "I'm just trying to help you. One cop to another."

"Am I the only suspect for this?"

"Whaddya mean?"

"Is there anyone else you're looking at for this crime?"

"Maybe."

"How did my name come up?"

"You were identified by a witness."

"At the scene?"

"None of your damned business."

Stanton pushed the photo toward Parr. "I had nothing to do with this. Whoever told you I did is lying to you. Should I be asking for a lawyer or are you going to let me go?"

Parr glanced at the camera and jumped to his feet suddenly, knocking back his chair. He grabbed Stanton by the throat and squeezed, staring into his eyes, looking for the fear he was accustomed to seeing, but Stanton didn't respond. His passive gaze never wavered or broke eye contact. Parr let go and chuckled.

"Just kidding with you, Jon." Parr took the photo and held it inches from Stanton's face. "But I'm not going to let you get away with it. You're gonna fry for this. This ain't hippie-dippie California."

He turned and left, letting the door slam behind him.

29

Nearly an hour passed before Stanton heard footsteps in the corridor and the door opened.

Orson Hall stepped in and stood by the doorway. "Let's go, Jon."

Stanton followed him outside to a police cruiser with a uniform in the driver's seat. They stood on the sidewalk as Orson lit a cigarette and offered one to Stanton, who turned it down.

After three puffs, Orson spoke. "You're leaving right now, Jon. This has gone too far. I can't have detectives associated with my department kidnapped. Can you imagine how that's going to look in the papers?"

"I'm sorry. It was stupid of me to go in there without any backup."

"Backup nothing, Jon. You're not a cop out here. You put lives in danger by pulling that shit."

Stanton turned away and watched the traffic as the lunch crowd headed back to work, their cars seeming lethargic.

"What happened at the house?" Stanton asked.

"SWAT went in. They didn't find anything. They did get the ropes in the basement. Kept your hand locks, too. We'll send 'em to the lab. Other than that there was some furniture in a bedroom, and that's it."

"Who's the owner?"

He blew a long stream of smoke through his nose. "You don't need to worry about that."

"Orson, who's the owner?"

"Daniel and Emily Steed. It was a vacant rental property."

Stanton glanced away, processing the information. "I'm close. I can feel it. He didn't mean to take me there. He panicked and didn't know what else to do. He didn't kill me when he had the chance. He's losing his grip."

"I doubt that. I'm starting to accept that we're not going to catch this prick. He'll slip away and be picked up now and again for petty crimes. We'll have him in our jail and not even know it."

"It doesn't need to be that way. Give me a week."

"To do what?"

"Just follow up. You brought me out here for a reason. I'm too close. You can't cut me off now, Orson. He'll see it as a win if I leave. You can expect more from him."

"What do you mean 'cut you off'? You're too involved in this. It's just another case. You'll have a hundred more like it."

"No, something's different. I don't know how to explain it but something's different about this guy. If you don't help me, I'll stay here on my own. You know how stubborn I am."

Hall threw the cigarette butt down on the sidewalk and stepped on it. "One week. I'm booking your flight home now. That's all you get."

With a massive pounding headache, Stanton went back to his hotel. He went to the gift shop to pick up extra-strength ibuprofen and a Diet Coke before returning to his room. It had been cleaned well, and there were creases in the sheets from a recent wash and folding. He slipped off his shoes, turned off his phone and got into bed without taking off his clothes.

When he woke three hours later the headache had turned into a migraine. His vision was filled with colored dots, and the pain came in waves that emanated down his neck and into his back. He suffered from migraines since he was a child. He had been to every specialist his parents could find—one even suggested that a hyperactive spleen might have been responsible for the migraines—but in the end, no one could find anything wrong with him.

He lay in bed almost an hour, his eyes closed and the blinds drawn. He calmed his breathing and pretended that a cooling relief was washing over him, starting with his head. Slowly, the migraine began to fade then went away.

Stanton rose from the bed and turned his phone back on. He had two messages from Mindi, one from his ex, and one hang-up. He dialed his ex.

"Hi," she said.

"Hey."

"I called a while ago. Where you been?"

"Busy. How are the boys?"

"They're good. Matt's here. Do you want to talk to him?"

"Yes." Stanton heard shuffling, followed by the unmistakable voice of his oldest son. His mother asked him to speak to his father, and he asked, "Do I have to?"

Stanton felt pain in his chest. It was so pronounced, so sudden, that he could've sworn it was a physical pain, although he knew it wasn't.

"Mel, it's okay if he doesn't want to. You don't need to force him."

"It's just that he's going over to Rhett's house and they need to get ready for their Little League practice and—"

"It's okay. You don't need to spare my feelings. What eleven-year-old wants to spend time talking to his old man? I'll call back tomorrow."

"You sure?"

"Yes."

"Okay. Oh, I almost forgot—the reason I was calling was because I need the child support check early this month. We're going on a trip and I'll need some extra cash."

"That's not what the check's for, Mel."

"They're coming with me. We're going on a cruise for seven days. They'll have a blast."

"What about school?"

"It's just a week. They'll be fine. I'll get their homework before we leave and we can do it on the boat." There was a long pause, and Stanton could tell she was walking into another room. "This hasn't been easy on them, Jon. They're really confused. Matt's old enough that he can read the newspapers. Kids at school tease him. There was an article in the *Trib* saying you've had more shootings than any detective at the police department. Matt remembers Eli, too. He still calls him Uncle Eli, and the other day he asked why he hurt all those girls. What do I tell them, Jon? Do you even have the faintest clue what your job does to them?"

"What do you want me to say to that?"

"Nothing. I'm just telling you when kids tell the boys that their dad's friend who came over every week and took them to baseball games is a murderer, they don't know how to respond."

Stanton could feel the frustration and anger as he spewed out, "I see things people aren't meant to see. Crackheads who stick their babies in the microwave 'cause they won't stop crying. Pedophiles who rape children in the aisles of grocery stores. I see that every day, and everybody I see on the street tells me that the government has too much power, that I'm intruding in their lives. And when the junkie who's been up for a week on a meth binge comes breaking into their home in the middle of the night, suddenly I'm a hero. I'm the knight in shining armor only to be forgotten as soon as the memory fades."

"I don't feel bad for you, Jon. I told you to quit a thousand times. You broke up our family because of that job. I hate that job." She hesitated. "And I'm learning not to care about you. I know I'm going to get a call from the department telling me you're lying in the morgue, and they need me to come identify you. I'm preparing for that. I'm treating you as if that's already happened. I'm sorry, but I don't know any other way to do it." A man's voice spoke to her, sounding as if it came from another room. "I gotta go. Call tomorrow in the afternoon."

There was a click, and she was gone. Stanton hung up the phone. The migraine had returned and he lay back down, staring blankly up at the ceiling as drums rumbled to life outside his window from a street show.

30

Cal Robertson walked slowly on the treadmill, watching a presidential debate on CNN. He flipped through the channels for a few seconds as he wiped his face with a towel then he turned off the television. The country club gym was nearly empty at ten o'clock at night. That was his favorite time to be there.

He walked over to a rack of weights. He took the five-pound barbells and did a few lateral raises to work his shoulders. He had recently had rotator cuff surgery, and the physical therapy was going slowly. Still, he had to admit, it was staggering how far medicine had come.

He finished three sets and headed to the showers. Another man, a banker named Damien Woodward, was already there. Cal said hello to him as he undressed and went to the shower next to him.

"How's the gambling business?" Woodward asked.

"Maybe I should be asking you that."

Woodward laughed and went on to describe the sex he'd had that weekend with his twenty-four-year-old girlfriend, despite being well into his late sixties. Cal listened politely as he washed up. Sex interested him only to a certain degree. He didn't let it run his life. It was sloppy and awkward as far as he was concerned. What was a few moments of pleasure compared to the thrill of making money or buying a rival company? In comparison, sex was fleeting and a waste of strength.

Cal dressed in a sweatsuit with a white stripe down each leg and put on his new sneakers. He left the gym, nodding good-bye to the teenaged girl behind the counter and climbed into his Lincoln Town Car that was parked near the front entrance. He pulled out onto Desert Foothills Drive heading back into the city.

His home was twenty minutes away and he rolled down the windows for the drive. He pulled into a gated community and drove up a winding driveway. He scanned an access card at another gate which opened with a loud, sustained creak. He would have to make sure to have that fixed.

His home was situated on two acres of lush grass and red rocks. Occasionally he saw ducks and geese in the small pond in front of the house, the geese driving away the ducks with their larger girth.

The attached three-door garage held his prized automobiles, each imported and specifically tailored to his tastes. He pressed the button on his visor and one of the doors began to rise. Then he heard the first pop.

A sound like a buzzing bee whizzed past his ears. At first he looked around to make sure an actual bee hadn't made its way into his car. The clinks against the frame of the car drew his attention to the right, where he saw small flashes in the darkness. He still wasn't sure what was happening until a slug smashed through the passenger window and punctured the car seat.

He screamed as shards of glass flew over him. Cal unlocked the driver's side door and fell out as another slug hit the tire, releasing a loud hiss. His hands were bloody and he felt the sting of glass embedded in his face. He crawled toward the open garage. He waited a moment at the hood of his car then got up on his knees. He ducked his head underneath the car and saw a pair of legs in jeans running toward him. Adrenaline and fear coursed through him. His hands were trembling as he rose and ran for the garage.

A burning sensation in his shoulder preceded an impact that knocked him off his feet. He felt no pain at first, and he managed to rise and get into the garage. He ran to the steps leading inside and pressed the button to lower the garage door. It began its slow, ponderous closing, and he saw the shooter pick up speed as they sprinted towards him.

The shooter was close, no more than a few dozen feet away, and the garage door had another couple of feet to lower. He couldn't make out a face but he saw the man raise his weapon and fire. The slug dented the thick garage door.

A hand reached under the door as it neared the ground. But the door's descent didn't slow, and the hand pulled away as the door pressed against the cement. Cal's heart fell into his stomach and his knees buckled. He sat on the steps leading to the kitchen door behind him and began to weep. Blood poured from his shoulder though there was no pain. Then he heard the sound of his car door opening, and a moment later the garage door started to rise.

He jumped up, panicked, and turned the doorknob. He had left it unlocked as he always did. He shut the door behind him and locked it. Past the living room, a staircase led up to the bedrooms. He ran for the stairs, his legs burning, and sprinted up them as quickly as he could. He heard an impact against the kitchen door. The shooter broke in.

He made his way to the master bedroom on the right.

His wife looked up from the book she was reading. "Cal? What's all that noise?"

Without answering he ran to the closet and flipped on the light. In the back corner was a gun safe and he put in the combo —the date he had officially made his first million. He took out a Smith & Wesson .44 caliber handgun. It was large and heavy; he had bought it immediately after seeing *Dirty Harry*.

"Cal! What the hell is going on?"

As footsteps ascended the stairs, Cal ducked and pointed the weapon. He had never fired it. He hadn't even held it since the day he bought it. Now, heavy in his hands, it felt like the best friend he had ever had.

His wife screamed as a figure in a black coat rounded the corner. The man pointed his weapon at Cal's wife just as a boom echoed through the home, as if a car had collided into the house. Cal flew off his feet and the gun dropped to the floor.

The man was lying on his back; a spray of blood covered the hallway. Cal managed to get to his feet and pick up the man's weapon. He held it with both hands as he walked over to the man. He was younger, maybe in his thirties, and the large wound in his chest was making a sucking noise. Cal aimed the barrel at the man's head as his eyes glazed over and went blank.

He lowered the weapon, exhausted, his whole body in pain. He turned to his wife who was sitting in shock on the bed.

"Don't just fucking sit there," he said. "Call the police."

31

Alma Parr sat on his balcony, nursing a whiskey and reading news reports about Jon Stanton on his iPad. The newspapers, generally, had treated him neutrally at the beginning of his career, but Parr noticed that a pattern had emerged as time wore on. Certain reporters always treated him well and certain ones always treated him poorly. Clearly he had developed a close relationship with some of them. Parr had never been able to accomplish such a feat. Reporters nourished themselves with misery and it made him sick. He treated them the way they treated everyone else; as a means to an end. On days when he didn't need a particular end, the reporters went for a rough ride.

There was a knock at his door.

"Come in," he shouted. He didn't remember if he had invited Karen over, but he knew she occasionally liked to pop in unannounced. The door opened and Orson Hall stepped in, a six-pack under his arm.

He came out onto the balcony and sat in the chair next to Parr.

"You know," Orson said, "my granddaddy worked in a factory during Prohibition. I sometimes wonder where I'd be now if he'd had the balls to be a bootlegger."

"My grandfather spent the last ten years of his life in federal prison. I doubt he thought it was worth it."

Orson looked at his whiskey. "Mind if I get one of those?"

"Help yourself."

Orson went inside to the bar. As he fixed himself a drink, he hummed and Parr could tell he was already drunk.

"Heard you had a meeting with the chief about our boy," Parr said.

"Stanton?"

"Yeah."

"Chief's nervous. Just trying to cover his ass." Orson came out and sat back down, holding a glass filled to the brim with whiskey. "You should invite some women over."

"You sure you up to it?"

He shrugged. "Guess not."

"Can I ask you somethin'? Why'd you bring Stanton out here anyway? Jay and Javier are two'a the best we got. Hell, I coulda taken a crack at this case. Seems like you didn't really wait."

"It happened over two weeks ago and we had nothin'. I was getting desperate."

"Why?"

He waved his hand. "Powerful forces behind this one. And they want it solved yesterday." He took a gulp of the whiskey. "Bastard's somethin' else, though, Al. I'm telling you."

"He didn't seem like shit to me."

"Looks are deceptive. See, you, you're an open book. What you see is what you get. You wear your heart on your sleeve and because of that you think everyone else does, too. That's not the way it works. Stanton looks like a choirboy on the outside, but inside... I don't know what he is. A monster maybe."

"You sure we're talking 'bout the same guy?"

"You know how I met him? It was a forensics seminar. One of those bullshit things that you're gonna have to start goin' to when you start moving up. There were six speakers and Jon was the last one. By the time he came in, he could tell we were all half asleep anyway, so he didn't lecture. He had us show him something, any item we had, like a pen or a badge, and he told us that he would leave the room and we were supposed to hide it anywhere we wanted. He came back a few minutes later, and damn if he didn't find it every single time without a word from any one of us."

"Was it a small room?"

"No, auditorium. We even had one'a the guys sneak out and throw his away—it was a paper cup or something—in a trash bin outside, and he still found it. He said the dust by the door was kicked up and it wasn't like that when he left. That's how he knew. I never saw anything like it."

Parr considered this for a moment. "He's got a few records over at the SDPD. Most arrests, most convictions, most shootings."

Orson swallowed a few more gulps. "Follow up on what you got. You can count on the full support of the chief and me. I think he burned that body. I want him in cuffs and behind bars within the week. Can you get it done?"

"All I got is the word of a few cholos right now. I'm sure I can find more."

"You ever work Narcotics?"

"No."

"Here's what you do to bust those assholes: find some piece'a shit who will take fifty bucks to write an affidavit about drug activity in the house, or you go through their trash. Most junkies and dealers throw away the baggies they keep their product in. Supreme Court has said anything in the trash doesn't have the expectation of privacy or any protections. Most of 'em don't know that. Get the warrant and do the raid yourself. You and five or six guys you trust. If there's nothing there, you find something there."

"You telling me to throw down evidence?"

"Don't tell me you got a problem with that? You know how many brutality complaints I've fielded for you?"

"I've never thrown down. Never. If they didn't do it they shouldn't be arrested. It won't matter, though. I guarantee some drugs and weapons will turn up."

"Good. Good. Even better. Arrest and hit 'em hard. Have a line up and have 'em identify Stanton. Make sure you show 'em a picture of him first. I want a confession, too. But he'll never confess to you. Talk to Mindi."

"About what?"

"Get her to wear a wire around him."

"She'll never do it to another cop."

"You're her boss—boss her." He finished his whiskey and pointed his finger at Parr. "I want this fucker. He's humiliating us. Get him for me and your career here is going to be a good one."

Parr didn't say anything as Orson rose, picked up his six-pack and left the house.

32

Stanton woke, his hand on the firearm he kept on the nightstand. His eyes were wide open as he listened for the sound that had awakened him. He heard it again: knocking.

Holding his weapon behind his back, he rose, went to the door, and looked through the peephole. Mindi. He placed the gun down on top of the television and opened the door. She tried to say something then just ran at him and threw her arms around his neck. She kissed his cheek and pulled away.

"Sorry."

"It's okay. But you don't have to worry. I'm fine."

"I tried to see you at the station but Al wouldn't let me. They wanted some time alone with you they said."

"Yeah, we had our time alone."

"What do you mean?"

"They think I killed somebody. A burn victim in a car."

"That happened days before you flew out here."

"Apparently there's someone out there saying it was me."

"That's ridiculous. After everything you've been through they interrogate you?"

Stanton took his gun and put it back in the holster. "That's not important now. I need your help. Orson's forcing me to leave in a week. There's a lot we need to do before then. Have you heard anything from the tech people about that DVD?"

"Oh, yeah, they left a message saying to call them but I haven't done it yet."

Stanton checked the clock on the dresser. It was almost six in the morning. "How far a drive was the compound Freddy Steed lives in?"

"About an hour. Two if traffic's bad."

"Give me ten minutes to shower. Then we're heading out there."

Stanton showered, shaved and put on a fresh shirt and pants before fixing his hair. He looked at himself in the mirror for a while. The work had aged him past his thirty-four years. Wrinkles were beginning to appear around his eyes and he had found a few gray hairs. Stress. Humans were not supposed to experience the type of stress that modern men did. It was the true killer of civilizations, a quiet one that few suspected. Stress drove presidents and kings to madness and made entire nations fall. Stanton fought stress as best as he could, but in the quiet morning hours he sometimes woke with a pounding heart and butterflies in his stomach. He knew he wouldn't make it to retirement. He would have to quit soon or die doing it.

He stepped out of the bathroom and saw Mindi, still in uniform, lying on the bed, flipping through the channels.

"You can't wear that. We'll have to stop by your apartment and have you change."

"Why?"

"If these guys are real white supremacists they're also anti-government. Any representation of government will set them off. We're not cops today."

"What about our backup?"

"Call in for at least one unit but we're gonna have them park half a mile away from the compound. You ready to go?"

"Yup." She hopped off the bed.

They left the hotel and Stanton went to the valet to retrieve the Cadillac, but Mindi informed him that his Cadillac had been returned to the car rental agency. So they got into Mindi's squad car and pulled onto Las Vegas Boulevard.

"We need to find another car. Can we use your Jeep?"

"No, it's in the shop for the transmission. My sister has a decent car, though. She'd let us borrow it. She has clothes that could fit me, too."

"How far away does she live?"

"Twenty minutes. It's in North Vegas. Practically on our way."

Mindi left the strip and headed toward Heather Lakes Drive, where trailer parks sat to the right and used car dealerships on the left. The dilapidated park sat empty, except for a few homeless men drinking on the playground.

Mindi turned up a winding street and parked in front of an old stucco-and-brick apartment building.

"Do you wanna wait or come in?"

"I'll come in."

Mindi led him to the third floor, where she knocked on a door with chipped paint and a rusty doorknob. Stanton could hear kids screaming from inside.

A woman who somewhat resembled her, with the addition of perhaps thirty pounds and bleached-white skin, answered. "What you doin' here?" she asked.

"I need to borrow your car. And some clothes."

"What for?"

"It's for a case. I didn't want to drive all the way back. We'll pay."

"How much?"

"Fifty bucks."

"Hundred."

"Fine."

The woman fully opened the door and Mindi walked in, motioning for Stanton to follow. He stood against the wall as the woman shut the door. Mindi went into a bedroom and told him she would be out in a minute.

The woman was staring at him and Stanton noticed that the cigarette dangling from her fingers had the distinct odor of tobacco mixed with marijuana. Many people used the trick to make their pot last longer.

"So you a cop, too?" she asked.

"Yeah."

"Our daddy was a cop. We got different mamas but the same daddy."

"She didn't tell me that. Was he here in Vegas?"

"Yeah. He died when we was kids."

"Sorry to hear that."

She inhaled and then blew out a puff of smoke. "He busted some meth house and they started shootin'. He got hit in the neck. Died 'bout an hour later." Another drag off the cigarette. "Was your daddy a cop, too?"

"He was a psychiatrist, a shrink."

"I know what a psychiatrist is."

"I didn't mean it that way."

Two small children poked their heads out from the kitchen. Stanton waved and they disappeared.

"How many kids do you have?" he asked.

"Four. Little shits, all of 'em. You?"

"Two."

Mindi stepped out wearing jeans and a blue short-sleeved shirt.

Her sister eyed her. "Don't go ruinin' my clothes."

"I won't. Where're your keys?"

"Bowl on the TV."

Mindi grabbed them and reached into her purse. Stanton took out a hundred-dollar bill from his wallet and gave it to the woman.

"I got it, Jon."

"It's fine. We should get going, though."

"I'll be back after work," Mindi said. "Don't leave."

"I won't," she said.

They left the apartment and didn't speak until they were driving away. Stanton checked emails on his phone.

"You can say it," Mindi said.

"Say what?"

"That you didn't think I came from a family like that."

"Family like what? She was nice."

"She's a trainwreck. Those kids—she's not sure who the father is for any of them. She sells meth and other things on the side to pay her bills. Not in front of me but I know she does it."

"It's easy to judge other people."

"So, you don't judge the dirtbags you bust every day?"

"No."

"I call bullshit on that."

"It's not my place. It's between them and God."

Mindi pulled onto the interstate heading out to the desert. A semi nearly cut her off; she flipped off the driver then sped ahead and cut him off.

"Do you *really* believe in that... in religion?"

"Yes."

"So you really believe that the earth was created six thousand years ago?"

"No. A lot of it is allegory."

"Well, at least you're honest."

Stanton waited a few beats then said, "Your sister was talking to me while you were changing. She told me your father passed away when you were young, that he's the reason you became a cop."

"I don't know—I guess. I don't think about it much. It just seemed like what I wanted to do since I was a kid. Hey, there they are."

A police cruiser was waiting alongside the interstate. Mindi honked as she passed and the cruiser pulled into traffic and followed them.

They drove through empty desert. Stanton counted one rest stop and one gas station in fifty miles. They turned off the interstate onto a partially paved road and headed northeast. The land was barren, occasionally dotted by an abandoned car or motorhome. It was tough, desert country. The kind captured in early Western movies.

"There's a rumor," Mindi said, "that they used to do nuclear testing out here in the '50s. I've never seen any evidence of it but some of the old-timers on the force swear it. They say the government's covered it up because the radiation affected families who lived nearby."

They pulled off onto a dirt road that led them between two large hills. On the other side, a huge structure came into view. Several smaller buildings surrounded it and the compound was entirely walled in by a fence that Stanton guessed was probably nine or ten feet high.

"Tell the unit to wait for us here."

Mindi dialed a number on her phone. "Wait for us here... no, no. I don't think so.... Yes, I'm sure. We'll be fine.... Half an hour. ... Okay, okay. Bye." She took a deep breath. "I've never done anything like this before."

"You're going to be waiting in the car."

"What? No, I can help. What if something goes down?"

"Nothing's going to happen. They're probably going to have a few choice words for me and send me on my way. Just in case, I want you in the car. Leave it running. If you hear anything out of the ordinary you pull away as fast as you can and call the unit to come meet you."

"I think this is a stupid decision, Jon. I really do."

"If it is then I'm only exposing myself to it. Park here."

She pulled to a stop in front of the gate. A large Confederate flag was draped over it, next to a sign warning trespassers to stay away. Stanton stepped out of the car and shut the door behind him. He checked his watch.

"Half an hour. After that, call it in."

He turned toward the facility. The fence easily circled a quarter of a mile. The gate, made up of several interlacing steel bars, was the only place to pass through. He peered in. A couple of women were tending to a massive garden. A row of Jeeps, motorcycles, and trucks took up a wall on the south side. A pirate flag flew over the entrance to one of the smaller buildings.

There was no intercom at the gate. He glanced around and

saw a foot and a half of space underneath the gate. He got on his belly and crawled in. He stood up on the other side and went to dust himself off but changed his mind. He began walking toward the women in the garden. They stopped talking as soon as they saw him. One of them ran to the building behind them, and the other stood and faced him.

"Who are you?"

"My name's Jon." He took out his badge. It said San Diego Police Department on it, but he figured no one would look too closely. "I'm with the police."

Several men rushed out of the building the woman had run into. Some looked like stereotypical neo-Nazis with shaved heads and red shoelaces on black boots. Others looked as though they could have been hanging out at any mall in the country, wearing polo shirts and jeans with Nike sneakers. A younger one in a white polo shirt stepped forward. The woman shouted to him that Stanton was a police officer.

"What you want, policeman?"

"I just need a couple minutes of your time and I'll be outta here."

Two men came out of a building holding assault rifles. The young one waved them back. They stood their ground but lowered the rifles.

"What would I wanna talk to you about?"

"Fredrick Steed. I understand that he lives here. I need to speak to him about his parents."

Another man came outside. He was tall and gaunt, with blond hair that hung to his shoulders. He appeared incredibly fit and his countenance wasn't angry like the others. In fact, he was smiling.

"Get outta his face, Curly Boy," he said to the young man. He walked over to Stanton and held out his hand. "I'm Brody."

"Jon. Are you in charge here?"

"Nobody's really in charge but I'll speak for us. We can talk inside."

Stanton followed as the crowd separated to let him through.

The men and women glared at Stanton as he passed and he saw that many of them had the dark ink and unsteady tracing of prison tattoos. Several of the women held babies in their arms.

Brody led Stanton into the building with the pirate flag. It was a bar. On the north side sat the actual bar, packed and messy. There were tables with worn leather chairs, Ping-Pong and pool, arcade games and several dartboards. A massive television taking up a wall in the back was turned to a college rugby game. Brody got behind the bar and poured himself absinthe and lime juice. He poured Stanton one as well. He took it to be polite and placed it in front of him.

"I appreciate you talking to me."

Brody took a sip. "I can tell pure Aryan blood when I see it. So what do you want?"

"I'm here about Fredrick Steed. Is he here right now?"

"What do you want with Freddy?"

"It's about his parents."

"Oh, yeah. Yeah, he didn't talk much about that but we heard."

"Nobody's interviewed him yet. It won't take long."

He finished his drink in two gulps. "Freddy took off 'bout a week ago."

"Do you know where?"

Brody shook his head. He sat up on the bar, letting his legs dangle off the edge. "People come'n go here. Some of us are permanent but most of the people stay a few weeks and move on. Or they get busted and spend some time in the can and come back after. Or don't. Freddy hung out here 'cause he and Tyler were really tight. They spent some time together in the can for burglaries."

"Is Tyler here?"

"Yeah, he's here."

"Do you mind if I speak with him?"

He watched him in silence. "Now, I start letting the police talk to my men, people start asking questions. They think I'm weak, that I gave into 'the man.' But if you were to gimme something, then I could say that I got the better deal."

"That sounds like the words of a leader in a place that's not supposed to have any."

Brody grinned. "You wanna deal or not?"

"What do you want?"

"Simple thing, brother. Nothing you wouldn't do anyway."

"What is it?"

"There's a shipment of coke coming in on Saturday to the Black Guerrillas. You hearda them?"

"Vaguely."

"That coke, they're gonna sell that and buy themselves some weapons. None of that Tech-9 shit. They want some serious gear. And let's just say we've had some run ins and I'd prefer they not have that. I want you to send a word to the Narcs."

"There's no guarantee Narcotics will move on it. That's not how government works. If someone can't take the credit in the newspapers they won't do anything about it."

"I know. That's why I didn't ask you to bust it. I just said to pass the word on. There's a captain in Metro named Stewart. You pass it on to him and he'll move on it. I'd bet my nuts he'll move on it. Used to be part of the Aryan Brotherhood before he put on a badge."

"I don't understand why you couldn't just tell him yourself."

Brody shrugged. "I got my reasons. That's all I'm asking, brother. Simple."

"Okay. You have my word, I'll tell him."

"Good. Curly Boy'll get you the address and the time of the drop." He hopped off the bar. "I'll get Tyler."

Stanton ran his fingers over his firearm and looked over the room. He wasn't entirely certain that someone wasn't about to rush in with an assault rifle. He waited a few minutes, and when no one came, he relaxed a little. He pushed away his glass and stood up. He walked over to the bookshelf against the wall and browsed the titles. They were mostly books about Nazi Germany, biographies of Hitler and Stalin, and technical manuals on warfare and farming.

The door opened and a slim young kid walked in. He couldn't have been older than twenty, and looked frightened. He stood near the entrance as Brody looked at him and said, "You got five minutes, Jon. Then I'm gonna need you to leave."

After Brody had left, Stanton walked toward the young man. He would have offered to shake hands, but Tyler's eyes were darting around the room and he was jittery. Stanton could smell a stink that he knew well. It was somewhere between burnt light bulbs and glue that had been set on fire—the smell of recently cooked and smoked meth.

"How are you, Tyler?"

"Fine. Fine, I'm fine." He reached to the back of his head and scratched furiously. "Brody said you wanted to talk to me about Freddy. He was a good guy. We was at HD together."

"Is that a prison?"

"Yeah. Yeah, he was a good guy. We was cellies. I don't know what happened to him."

"Did he just leave one day?"

"Yeah. Yeah, didn't say nothing to nobody. He just took off."

"How long ago was that?"

"Few days."

"Brody said he left last week."

"Yeah, that's what I meant. He left last week. I don't know. I'm not good with time," he said with a slight chuckle. "Anyways, he ain't here."

"Is there a way you can reach him?"

"No. I don't know where he is. He's gone."

"Yeah, you said that." Stanton watched him as Tyler glanced around the room and tried desperately to avoid his eyes. Stanton ran his eyes along the door and over the walls. Behind the bar, a door led to the back. It was open a few inches and Stanton could see the shoulder of someone who was listening in. Stanton took out his card and a pen from his pocket. He wrote "call me later if you can help" on the back of the card and set it on a table. "Doesn't sound like you know anything, Tyler. I appreciate you speaking to me, though."

"Yeah," he mumbled.

Stanton went past him and toward the door. He looked back and saw Tyler grab the card and slip it into his pocket. Outside, Brody was standing with his arms folded, a smile on his face. The men with the assault rifles had disappeared and everyone in the commune had seemingly gone back to whatever they were doing before Stanton's arrival.

"Get what you need?" Brody asked.

"No, he didn't know anything. Is there anyone else I can talk to that you can think of?"

"Sorry, brother. Freddy kept to himself mostly. Tyler was his only friend."

"Well, I'm grateful just the same."

"Curly Boy wrote the address down on this." He handed Stanton a slip of paper.

Stanton realized for the first time that Brody couldn't read. "Thanks. The narcotics detective was named Stewart, right?"

"Yeah. Ian Stewart. White dude, goin' bald. Kinda greasy lookin'."

"All right. I'll give him this."

As Stanton walked toward the gates, his back felt itchy. He was nervous that one of them might open fire, although he knew that wouldn't actually happen. For whatever reason, Brody needed him to talk to Stewart.

Curly Boy opened the gate and waited until Stanton stepped outside to shut it. "Don't you be comin' back now. We love us some piggy barbeque."

Mindi sat in the car, biting her thumbnail and spitting out little pieces through the open window. Stanton climbed in. She started the car and took off without saying a word.

"Well?" she said after they had put some distance between themselves and the compound.

"Doesn't look like we're going to be talking to Freddy."

"Why not?"

"Because I think he's dead."

33

It was nearly midnight when Alma Parr's cell phone woke him up. He had his ringtone set to the most soothing piece of music he could think of: Bach's *Ave Maria* for the harp. Regardless of how calm and relaxing the music was, it still jolted him awake. He grabbed the phone and looked at the screen. It was Javier.

"This better be good. I was in a hot tub with Jessica Alba."

"Home invasion on Cal Robertson good enough for you?"

"You're shitting me? Anyone hurt?"

"Just the intruder. Got a hole in his chest about four inches across."

"Text me the address. I'm coming right now."

Parr jumped up and went to the closet. He put on jeans and a tight black T-shirt before grabbing his badge and placing the chain around his neck. He put on his holster and firearm and took a leather jacket out of his closet before running out the door.

Within twenty minutes, he drove through the open gate into the enclosed community. The homes were worth millions of dollars but they didn't seem comfortable, just luxurious. The entire community represented the type of home meant to impress others, despite being unwelcoming to the owners themselves. Parr found the house and parked in the driveway. He slipped under the police tape across the front door and saw two uniforms trading notes in the living room.

"What genius put tape on the front door? Get that shit down and one of you stand out there. Reporters can slip under the tape."

"Al, up here."

Parr looked up the stairs where Javier stood at the top. He practically skipped up the steps two at a time. Off to the right, near a bedroom, assistants from the Clark County Coroner's Office were bagging up a body. The corpse was tall, around six foot four or six five, with a large black wound marking his chest like a decoration. Parr let the assistant zip up the bag and place it on a stretcher. A forensic tech went to work on the blood spatter across the wall, and Parr stepped over him into the bedroom. On a couch in a corner of the massive space, much larger than his living room and kitchen combined, Cal Robertson sat with his wife.

"Didn't know you were into making Swiss cheese, Cally boy."

Cal looked up, saw Parr, and cursed under his breath. "What are you doing here? I thought you got promoted."

"Oh, I'm never too busy for my favorite power broker. How's the casino business? Not making too many enemies I hope?"

Cal turned to his wife and gently placed his hand over hers. "Dear, do you mind if we talk in private for a minute?"

"Sure," his wife said. Parr could see the shock that had taken hold of her as she stood up and left the room. She stepped over the forensic tech without looking down at the large black stain taking up most of her hallway carpet.

"Didn't know you had it in you, you old bastard," Parr said.

"Fuck you, Alma. What is it with you anyway? You got a hard-on for me? You break into my charity event and arrest me like a street thug."

"You are a street thug. You're just a rich, old street thug. I heard you pled out on the public assistance fraud charge? Lemme ask you something: How is it that a rich prick like you thinks it's a good idea to get a few hundred extra dollars a month by lying on a worker's compensation claim? Was it the thrill?"

He became visibly upset. "I worked my ass off to get where I am, and the fucking government is gonna take half my money and give it to welfare whores in the ghetto? You better believe I'm gonna get as much of that back as I can."

Parr shook his head. "So," he said, looking back at the blood-stain, "what happened?"

"What does it look like happened? That cocksucker tried to kill me."

"Do you know him?"

"No. I was just pulling into my garage and he started shooting at me."

"Make any enemies lately? Other than the hundreds you already have?"

"I'll tell you exactly who did this. Bill fucking James. That sonofabitch thinks he can take me out? *Me*? Well, I'm not dead yet. I got something in store for him."

"Why would you think Bill James did this?"

"Oh, you want a story? I'll give you a story. It's the Cubans. They're opening back up. Back to business. Or that's the bullshit Bill gave us. He wants to spend almost a billion dollars building two casinos and hotels on the beaches in Havana. He says he needs half the money up front as a sign of good faith. Half! The crazy sonofabitch wants to give five hundred million dollars of our money to the Cuban government without so much as a handjob in return. And who the hell knows where the rest of the money's coming from. Well, the board didn't go for it, and I told him what he could do with his money."

"How do you know Cuba's opening up again?"

"Bill says he has some insider in the government, some bull-shit he fed us. We didn't buy it and he's mad as hell."

"If the board shot him down, what would he gain by taking you out?"

"There's two personalities on that board: Bill James and me. If they don't follow me, they'll follow Bill James."

Parr glanced around the bedroom. "Give Javier all the details. I'll pay Bill a visit."

"I want another detective on this case."

"Other than Javier? Why?"

"He's a spic. He'll only work hard enough not to get in trouble."

"You're the convicted felon, asshole. You don't want us to find who did this, then don't work with Javier. I'm sure Bill James will forget all about this little incident and not try anything else."

He turned away as Cal said something. Javier was playing with a toothpick near the bedroom door. Parr put his arm around his shoulders, and they walked out to the hallway and into the next bedroom, where it was quiet.

"You believe him?" Javier asked.

"I've had a lotta run-ins with him, and he's never once told me the truth about anything. He's as dirty as they come."

"Bill James, though... we had him for the Steed case."

"We didn't have anything but a motive. Cal's got at least a hundred people who would love to put a bullet in his head. You know how he got rich? He used to push junk penny stocks to retirees. He'd clean up on commission fees and leave them holding the bag when the stock plunged. He's a rat."

"We could just, you know, not worry about who did this."

"No, we're the law, no one else. We can't allow fuckers to go around executing people. Even pond scum like Cal."

"So where you wanna start?"

"Run the routine. Follow up on the body, the weapon, the ammo. He had to get here somehow, so get some uniforms out looking for abandoned cars and call the cab companies, too. See if anyone dropped him off."

"Guy's got a professional-grade suppresser on the tip of that gun. Not the homemade junk. Top of the line. He's probably not off the streets."

"Or someone's financing him. If he was a pro, he wouldn't have let some old man with irritable bowel syndrome blow his guts out. I'm thinking amateur. And if he's amateur, he left a trail for us to find who hired him. Once you find out who he is, make sure we go through bank accounts and safe deposit boxes."

Javier sighed. "Your wish is my command."

Parr left the house and got into his car. He looked at the mansion in front of him. It was a den of corruption and decadence. Cal had all this and he still risked prison to steal a few extra bucks from the government. Parr would never understand people like him.

34

Mindi had work to finish up before her shift ended, so Stanton was alone all morning. He performed his usual routine before going down to the buffet for breakfast. He sat at the table near the window and placed his phone in front of him. He was expecting a call, and he hoped it would come that day.

Out of the corner of his eye, as he took a bite of waffle with butter and syrup, he saw a young couple fighting. They were arguing about mundane things that they probably wouldn't remember the next day, as young people did. Stanton suddenly felt a sharp pang of loss as he thought about his ex-wife and the day they had gotten married. She had looked stunning, her exposed shoulders, tan and muscular, contrasting against the white dress. He thought of the day they had found out she was pregnant with their first son. They had gone out for ice cream but were so broke they could only afford one child-sized scoop to share. He thought of the day he received his doctorate from the University of Utah. She had saved all year to take him on a four-day vacation to Hawaii afterward.

He wondered what had happened to those times. They had flown by so quickly, like an arrow shooting away from him. They faded in the distance and were gone in an instant.

According to modern personality theory, every individual has a five-tier personality, and one trait dominates the personality matrix: openness to experience, neuroticism, conscientiousness, agreeableness, and extroversion. He understood that each individual could be categorized under one dimension only, even though he or she may have traits from others.

Those open to experience were artistic, creative, and full of ideas. They focused on the big picture and paid little attention to details. Neurotics worried and were moody, unable to control their emotions. They were always ruled by emotions like anger, fear, frustration and negativity. Conscientious personalities were organized and efficient, and got things done immediately, while agreeable personalities empathized with people and tended to be cooperative rather than combative. Extroverts were marked with a tendency to seek out stimulation, particularly stimulation from others. They were always the life of the party and could scarcely handle being alone.

Stanton believed that couples whose dimensions of personality were in line had the perfect relationships. Two neurotics would be mutually self-destructive and should not be together under any circumstance, but an extrovert would perfectly complement someone open to experience. Stanton had determined that he was an agreeable personality, and Melissa was the apex open personality, always willing to jump first and try new things. They helped each other in ways that they hadn't experienced before. Stanton was able to read her moods and respond accordingly. Melissa helped him to open up and be less preoccupied with the minds of others. Psychologically, they were a perfect fit.

Stanton had learned, however, that psychology didn't determine everything about what makes human beings who they are. There's something else that can't be quantified, deduced or analyzed: the soul. On a deep level, the deepest possible, he and Melissa simply were not soulmates. It had taken them more than a dozen years to figure it out.

Stanton's cell phone buzzed and he stared at it for a moment before answering. "Hello?"

"Yeah," a male voice said, "is this Jon?"

"This is Jon Stanton."

"This is, um, Tyler. Tyler from yesterday. You came and—"

"I remember you, Tyler. I'm glad you called."

"Yeah, yeah. Well, um, hey, do you have... I mean, can we talk?"

"Sure. Do you want me to pick you up?"

"No, no definitely not. I'm coming to Vegas to meet up with some people. Can you meet me in, like, two hours?"

"Sure. Where would you like to meet?"

"There's a restaurant called, um, Philly's. Yeah, Philly's. Wait... yeah, Philly's."

Stanton could hear the fatigue in Tyler's voice. The methamphetamine was wearing off. The binge he had been on for however many days was winding down, and his mind was a bowl of mush. "There's no deadline, Tyler. If you need to sleep first—"

"I don't need to sleep. No, I don't need to sleep. I just wanna get this over with."

"Okay. I'll meet you at Philly's in two hours."

"Okay, okay, better make it three hours. Okay?"

"Okay. See you there."

Stanton hung up the phone. He dialed Mindi's number.

"Hey, I'm meeting Tyler at Philly's in three hours," he told her.

"No way! I have a couple things to finish up. I'll be down to pick you up right after. Can you occupy yourself for a couple of hours?"

"I'll be fine. Don't worry. Could you do me a favor, though? I want to look through Marty Scheffield's file. Just the photos and the forensics reports."

"Not a problem. See you in a bit."

Stanton finished his breakfast and left a large tip before heading out to the casino floor. He put his hands behind his back, a position that he found comfortable for thinking, and walked circles around the casino. The ding of the machines and hoots and hollers of the players eventually melted away from his conscious thoughts, leaving only his voice in a slow, comforting monotone, organizing the bits of evidence.

Tyler had something extremely important for him. In neo-

Nazi organizations, cooperating with the police was a certain death sentence. He wouldn't do it lightly, or if he had irrelevant information. But something else was bothering Stanton: Marty Scheffield's death.

Despite having known him for only a short while, Stanton had liked Marty. He was open and had no deceit in him, which was a rare trait. Stanton hadn't really dealt with Marty's death. It was in the back of his mind, processing with the other bits of information he'd gathered during his time in this city. He felt he owed Marty something: convicting the man who had ended his life.

Within an hour his eyes were watering from the cigarette smoke and he had to go outside. He walked down the street, absently staring at the massive man-made constructions of Venice, Paris, New York, the Pyramids and old Hollywood. A giant screen was playing a video of a magician hypnotizing a couple into thinking they were dogs.

He passed Mandalay Bay, crossed the street, and went down the other side. It was early morning—far earlier than he would have liked to have been up—but the people were still getting drunk at the casino bars. Street peddlers were attempting to hand out pornography. Two women in mini-skirts and fishnet stockings walked out of a hotel in front of him. One commented on how repulsive the man she had just had sex with was.

When he returned to the Mirage, Mindi was there waiting for him. He climbed into her car and she handed him a Diet Coke as she pulled away onto Las Vegas Boulevard.

"Got what you wanted." She reached into her backseat, grabbed a file, and handed it to him.

Inside the file a paperclip held over a dozen enlarged, neatly stacked photos. The first was the image of the kicked-in window in Marty's basement. The next was of the glass that had spread over the carpets. The rest were different angles of Marty's position and his head wound. The two final photos were of cushions that had been thrown on the ground in the living room and a chest of drawers in the bedroom, all its contents emptied onto the floor.

Stanton flipped through the forensic reports. Three techs had spent a total of thirty-four hours in the house, an amount of time reserved only for the loss of one of their own. They had found almost nothing—no dirt, debris transfer, fingerprints or shoe prints. No fibers, DNA or even gunpowder residue except on Marty's skull.

"Isn't that weird?" Mindi asked, not taking her eyes off the road. "They didn't find anything but those drawers and the cushions. You think there was a struggle?"

"All the drawers wouldn't be pulled out in a struggle. They would've just knocked the whole thing over." Stanton closed the file. "He was looking for something. The fact that the rest of the house wasn't a mess means I interrupted him."

"What was he looking for?"

"I don't know. But if I interrupted him, it means it might still be there."

Mindi's phone rang. "Hello? Oh, hey.... Yeah, yeah.... Lemme ask." She turned to Stanton and said, "That's the lab. They're wondering when we want to come see what they found on that DVD you got from the Steed's house."

"Anytime."

"We'll be there at five o'clock tonight," she said. "Really? Can't you stay later than that? ... Okay, well, we'll be by at two then."

"Computer guys don't work long hours."

"We're lucky just to see them. Their government contracts are the lowest-paying contracts they have and we usually have to wait until they're done with their regular clients' work to get anything. They did a special favor for us because the CFO or somebody went to business school with Daniel Steed."

She drove for another ten minutes through areas filled with cookie-cutter homes and strip malls. One strip mall caught Stanton's attention. It consisted of a tattoo parlor, alternative clothing stores, a secondhand store and a vinyl record shop. Two girls, no older than eighteen, were standing on a corner near the buildings; wearing shorts and tank tops, smoking while cars honked at them.

Mindi finally came to a stop in front of a house that had been turned into a makeshift restaurant. A worn sign hanging over the front porch read PHILLY'S. The patio was packed tightly with customers. Stanton and Mindi got out and walked up the steps to the interior, which still looked like the living room of an old house. The hostess sat them in a semicircular booth in the corner.

"Well, we're right on time. I can't imagine a meth-head's gonna be punctual."

"Probably not," Stanton said.

"Mind if we order an appetizer? I'm starving."

They ordered potato skins with cheese and sour cream and two apple juices. Philly's served peanuts for free, and Stanton picked at them slowly and chewed without noticing the taste.

"You still here?" Mindi asked.

"What?"

"You looked like you were a million miles away."

"I was just thinking. Wondering if Marty would still be alive if I'd never come out here."

"Hey, you cannot think like that. That bullshit will eat you up. You surprised that guy and stopped whatever he was doing which means he would've done it anyway, with or without you. Don't beat yourself up over this." She stuffed half a potato skin into her mouth and wiped her lips with a napkin. "Can I tell you something? I feel like you were pissed at me because I wasn't always nice to Marty. You don't know the whole story."

"What is the whole story?"

"Before the accident... well, he was an asshole. He was always hitting on me and grabbing me. He cornered me once in his office after hours and tried to make out with me. When I was drunk at a New Year's party... when I was drunk at a New Year's party he tried to take advantage of it. He got my pants down and I screamed so loud that he got off and left, but a few more drinks and I would've been out of it. And he would've done it. He was always coming into the women's showers. I never saw it, but I heard from people that he would bust hookers just to get blow-jobs from them and then let them go.

"After the accident, he was a lot different. It was like he got his innocence back or something. But I couldn't forget what he was like before. I was never able to forgive him."

"I'm sorry. I didn't know."

"We all make mistakes."

"Yeah."

"Do you ever think you made the wrong choice? That you shoulda just stuck to the academic world?"

"Sometimes. I think everyone second-guesses their career at some point. It definitely would've been easier on my marriage. But there was something about it. I don't know. It was like a cave. People in academia seclude themselves. I think they do it on purpose. They don't want to know what's going on in the real world or deal with its problems."

"My mom always pushed me to become a nurse. She thought that being a cop was only for men. She was really one of those people who thought men do some things, women do others, and that's the way we're born. I hated that because she would never come to my baseball games or wrestling matches."

Stanton grinned. "You wrestled?"

"Hell yes I wrestled. I kicked ass at it, too. If they had a women's wrestling team at UNLV, I would've definitely been on it." She suddenly looked disturbed, as though an unwanted thought had pushed its way into her mind. "You seem like a really nice guy, Jon. I wish—"

"Officer Jon."

Stanton looked up and saw Tyler. He appeared worse than he had yesterday, as if he'd already aged. His skin was green and sagging, and he had dark circles under his eyes. He sat down at the booth and leaned his head back against the cushions.

"Do you want something to eat?" Stanton asked.

"Yeah, man. Definitely. I'll take a burger, some tacos, and fries."

Stanton called the waiter over and ordered. After the waiter left, Stanton waited a few moments before speaking again. "What was it you wanted to talk to me about, Tyler?"

"First off, man, you can't bring my name into this. I'm fuckin' serious. They will cut off my balls and feed 'em to me."

"We never met. I promise you."

"Brody and them, they was the ones that did Freddy."

"They killed Fredrick Steed?" Mindi chimed in. "Why?"

"They was paid to do it. A lotta money I guess."

"Who paid them?" Stanton asked.

"I don't know. Brody talked to 'em. They didn't tell me until they was gonna do it 'cause they knew we was tight. When you spend time in a cell, you grow tight like we was. Freddy wasn't bad. He didn't deserve to go out like that. Check this out, though —they made me record it."

"On what?"

"My cell phone."

"Do you have it here?"

"Yeah." He pulled out his phone and fiddled with it for a few seconds. He turned it toward Stanton.

The screen was dark at first. An interior light came on, revealing a figure in the driver's seat of a car. His hands were tied to the steering wheel with a thin rope and a piece went around his neck and wrapped around the car seat. Even though his eyes were bulging from being choked and his cheeks were puffy and red, Stanton could see the countenance of the little boy from the video he had watched.

Brody came into view. "You see what happens when you fuck with the Brotherhood?"

He poured lighter fluid over Freddie's face then emptied a gas can over him. Freddie was suffocating from the fumes and coughing violently. Brody threw the can into the passenger seat and pulled out a book of matches. Freddie pleaded through his coughs and wheezing. Brody grinned and threw a lighted match into the car. He tossed in a handful of something small that clinked against the dashboard: they were teeth. Stanton knew they had pulled his teeth to prevent identification.

The intense light from the flames made the screen go white. Freddie's muffled screams made the speaker crackle. Stanton could hear Tyler swearing, yelling and crying. The video ended.

"You stood by and watched while they did that to your friend?" Mindi asked.

"There was like twenty people there and everybody's got guns. What was I supposed to do?"

"You were supposed to stop them. You're a coward."

"Mindi," Stanton said softly. His eyes locked on hers briefly; she exhaled loudly and sat back in her seat, folding her arms. "Tyler," he said turning toward the young man, "I need your phone."

"What for?"

"I need to authenticate the video and make copies. I'll get it back to you as soon as possible."

"What am I gonna do without a phone? I need my phone."

Stanton pulled the phone out of his reach. "I'll pay you for it. Enough to get a new phone, but I need to take this one with me."

"Well, I ain't gonna be in trouble, right? I mean, I came to you guys and brought you the video and everything."

"I'll do everything I can to protect you."

"That don't sound like I'm not getting in trouble. You promised you'd keep my name out of it."

"No prosecutor is going to pursue a case against you for—"

"Pursue a case against me!" he shouted. "Fuck you. You fucking said you wouldn't say my name."

"I will do everything—*we* will do everything we can to protect you. If I have to, I'll find another way. I keep my promises."

Tyler stood up and pushed his middle finger into Stanton's face. "Fuck you!" He stormed out of the restaurant.

"That went pretty well," Mindi said.

Stanton tucked the phone into his pocket. "He's going to have to testify in court against Brody. They'll need him to lay the foundation for the video."

"He's not going to like that."

"If they're smart, they'll give the case to the Feds to prosecute under RICO. I'll bet Tyler knows everything about their drug trafficking and prostitution rings. The Feds'll give him immunity and a new life somewhere else. He can start over."

"There's no starting over for them, Jon. He can be a meth addict in Billings, Montana, as easily as Las Vegas."

"It'll at least give him a chance."

The food arrived. Stanton took out some cash and left it on the table. "Take it with us. I need to see your captain."

35

Parr was sitting at his desk, filling out a report, when Jay knocked.

"Come in," he shouted. No one came into his office without asking first. He had established that rule the day he'd been made captain.

"Cap, we got a hit on the home invasion in Cal's case." Jay sat down across from him and flipped through a file until he found the document he was looking for. "Seryoga Melikov. Thirty-three, a Russian immigrant with a rap sheet longer than my cock."

"That wouldn't take more than a couple charges."

Jay smirked and went on. "Lives in Trenton, New Jersey, and —get this—flew out to Las Vegas the day before he broke into Cal's house. There's even a video of him almost punching out one of the female desk attendants at the terminal because they bumped his flight a few times. He got cited for disorderly conduct and threw the citation in the trash before boarding his plane."

"Sounds like a peach. What else?"

"Got a few strong-arm robberies. We talked to his girlfriend— well, his ex-girlfriend. He put her head through a glass door and she dumped him after that. She said he's an asshole with a gun. Apparently he slept with the thing."

"Did she say why he came to Vegas?"

"He wasn't talking to her at the time, but she'd heard from someone else that he was pulling a robbery job out here."

Parr leaned back in his chair and put his feet up on the desk. "Did you call the PD over in Trenton?"

"Yeah, no ties to the Russian mob. They basically said he was a low-level hood known for break-ins."

"That doesn't sound like a pro. That sounds like someone making their bones for the first time."

"Who would hire an amateur to take out someone like Cal Robertson?"

"Someone who's never hired a gun before or hasn't done it in a long time. What about his bank accounts?"

"I was gonna follow up on that now. I wanted to see you about this first."

"Make sure to look for any large recent deposits. I'm not expecting a check, but maybe we can trace some of those bills if the bank's got numbers."

"I'm on it," Jay said before he got to his feet and left.

Parr was about to return to his reports when his door opened again, and Jon Stanton walked in. Mindi was behind him, saying something about knocking.

"What do you want?"

"You need to see this." Stanton pulled out the phone and played the video.

Parr watched it for a few seconds then jumped to his feet, pulled his firearm, and pointed it at Stanton's head. "Get the fuck on the ground, now!"

"Alma!" Mindi yelled.

"Hands up and on the ground!"

"He got the phone from someone who filmed it. I was there. That guy on the video is the one you want. It's the Aryan Brotherhood. Jon had nothing to do with it."

Alma didn't move.

Mindi stepped forward and put her hand on the gun, lowering it. "Alma, I was there. He had nothing to do with it. You were wrong."

Parr felt his face twinge with anger. "He's playing you, Mindi."

"No, he's not. I know you got it in your head that he's your guy, but whoever told you that was lying. Watch the video again and turn up the sound. You'll hear the guy's voice on the camera. It's his phone. His name is Tyler."

Stanton said, "And I just handed you all his text messages and contacts. The man on the video is named Brody. If you're gonna go after him, you'll need SWAT. They got a compound and they're heavily armed. Most of them didn't look like they'd hesitate to shoot at cops."

Parr replaced his firearm and sat down, taking a deep breath. "Get out of my office."

"Alma, what the hell is the matter with you?"

"It's fine," Stanton said. He started to walk out the door but turned at the last second. "The guy who made that, Tyler—he's not a bad person. And you wouldn't have closed this without him."

"I woulda found him eventually," Parr said.

Stanton watched him a moment and then said, "Anger's a poison. It only hurts you. You want to hurt the world, or me, or whatever, but you're only hurting yourself."

After Stanton left, Mindi stared at Parr.

"What?" he asked.

She shook her head and made a sound as if she were disgusted then followed Stanton.

As the door shut, Parr played the video again. He sighed then picked up the phone and dialed the number for tactical to arrange for SWAT.

Stanton was silent as they rode to the laboratories of Constance Digital, which were in a secluded business park located on over an acre of property. Complete with trees, two basketball courts, statues of people Stanton didn't recognize and a Pizza Hut on the first floor, it looked like something a college student would design. After Mindi parked, she and Stanton went to the main entrance where someone at the front desk buzzed them in. A large man in a wrinkled shirt and a dirty tie handed them a clipboard and they signed in before the interior door clicked and opened.

The hallways were decorated like a dorm room. *Baywatch* posters and prints of *Star Wars* were framed in cheap black frames. A few handmade drawings were posted on the walls in between the vending machines, which lurked every couple dozen feet.

Mindi led Stanton to a room where three people were eating Chinese take-out. One of them, a thin man in wire-frame glasses, turned to them and quickly took a bite of his sweet-and-sour chicken before standing up and wiping his hands on his jeans.

"What's up, Mindi?"

"Nothing much. This is Jon."

"How are ya? I'm Mike Lupford. I'm the manager here."

The other two giggled.

"What? I am, technically."

"We're here about that DVD," Mindi said.

"Yeah, come on back."

They followed him to a door at the back of the room where he used a key to unlock the door. The room beyond was dark and cluttered with electronic equipment and four large monitors took up an entire wall. Mike sat down in front of the wall of monitors.

"Have a seat," he said.

They sat down behind him as he queued up the video. Stanton noticed he wasn't wearing any shoes.

"So," Mike said, "this actually wasn't written over, like you thought. It was just corrupted. It looked like someone did a sloppy job of trying to erase the data on the disc."

"Were you able to get anything?"

"Oh, yeah. This was total amateur work. They probably used some program they downloaded off the Internet. We used CNW V3 and got it back in a few minutes. Um, it's kinda graphic." He pressed a button and a video started to play on the monitors. "Here we go."

The scene was just a room at first, with a few items of furniture: a bed, a side table and a lamp. Then a figure came into view. It was a woman in see-through negligée. She was speaking to someone off camera.

"Can you get sound?" Stanton asked.

"No, sorry. That's pretty easy to wipe out. We couldn't get it back."

The woman slipped off her negligée. Her back was visible and hands ran up and down the length of her body. She got down on her knees for a few minutes before standing up and lying down on the bed.

She reclined flat on her back as a male came into view. He was nude, but the shot didn't capture anything above his chest. He settled on top of her and worked himself inside her. He thrust for a solid five minutes before working himself into a frenzy and stopping. They lay with each other for a few minutes afterward, then the man stood up and turned off the camera.

Stanton recognized the woman—it was Mrs. Steed.

Mindi looked at him. "That looked like—"

"It was."

"So the Steeds had a sex tape? Kinda fun for a couple their age I guess."

"Rewind the tape please, Mike… thanks… stop it right there." Stanton moved closer to the screen. He pointed to the man's hand on the bed. "When we lay our hands flat and force them to bear weight, the majority of the weight's placed on our dominant hand. Look at the indentations on the bed. The left is much deeper. This guy's left-handed. Daniel Steed was right-handed."

"You think she was having an affair?"

"Can you tell how old the video is?" Stanton asked Mike.

"Yeah." Mike typed into a keyboard in front of him and a window popped up over the video. It was dated four months before the Steeds were killed.

Stanton turned away from the video and paced slowly. "Why would she keep the tape in her house?"

"Maybe they were into that sorta thing? Big swinger community in this town. I wouldn't be surprised if they were all kinky. Or maybe she thought it was erased?"

"It would've been much more secure to just throw it away. Why do a poor job erasing it and then keep it?"

Mindi shrugged. "Can you make us a copy, Mike?"

"Done and done." He pulled out a copy he had already made and put it into a cover. After that, he took out another copy, put it into a cover, and placed it on the table in front of them. From the way Mike immediately turned away from it, Stanton could tell he was saving it for himself.

"We'll need all of the copies and the original."

"Oh," Mike said, "yeah, it's just, you know... she was kinda hot."

Mindi punched him in the arm. "Gross."

"What? She won't care."

Stanton collected all the discs and he and Mindi headed out of the building. When they were back in the car, Stanton held the disc between his fingers and flicked it up and down like a playing card as he stared out the window of the moving car. He wondered if Daniel Steed had ever watched the tape.

"So how do we find this guy?"

"If they checked into any hotels, I doubt they did it under their own names. But it wouldn't hurt to go through Emily Steed's credit card statements and see if there's anything on them. We could follow up on any hotels that get a hit and see if they have surveillance video from that day."

She was silent for a long while before she said, "So, you're leaving soon. Do you think we should give all this stuff to Jay and Javier?"

"We will, but not yet. I'm so close. I can feel him."

36

Night fell over Las Vegas and the city came alive like a great hibernating animal awakened by the pang of hunger. The streets were packed with luxury cars, limousines and SUVs just out of the carwash. On the sidewalks, crowds swarmed like ants over honey, and large swaths of people would suddenly divert into this or that casino to catch the latest show. Just above the cityscape the tram zipped between casinos, carrying those who were too drunk to walk or families who didn't want to push strollers through the crowds.

Above it all, Bill James sat sipping a Manhattan.

James blew smoke out of his nose then shouted, "Bring me a drink, will ya?"

The blonde dancer he'd spent the night with brought him a gin and tonic, gave him one more kiss, and left. He sipped his drink and lit another cigarette before he had even finished the one he was smoking. He didn't know how long he had been sitting there, staring at the lights, when the intercom buzzed in his suite.

"Mr. James?"

"Yes."

"Mr. Kamal and Mr. Henry are here to see you."

"Send them in."

A minute later, Raj and Milton walked in. They fixed themselves drinks and came out onto the balcony. Raj stood at the railing and looked down at the street below, while Milton relaxed in a leather chair and put his feet up on a footrest with gold-leaf trim.

"Who the fuck did you get, Milton? A fucking school teacher?"

"He came highly recommended. I'll send someone else. Someone more experienced."

"No, it's too late. I know Cal and he's gonna be prepared now."

Raj looked from one man to the other. "What're we talking about?"

James glanced at him then out over the city. Milton cleared his throat and took a drink. He slipped off his Italian loafers and crossed his legs.

"Wait, hold on," Raj said. "Tell me you're not talking about what I think you're talking about."

"We didn't want to get you involved," Milton said. "The fewer people who knew, the better."

"Bill, tell me he's kidding."

James wouldn't look at him.

"Bill, tell me he's kidding!"

"That's life sometimes, kid. It'll have you by the balls and you gotta fight your way out."

"What are you talking about? Are you crazy? Cal's on the board. You've known the guy for thirty years."

"It wasn't an easy choice to make."

"No shit it wasn't an easy choice to make." Raj shook his head and began pacing frantically around the balcony. "You put the whole company in jeopardy. We got seven thousand employees. If shareholders lost faith in you, our stock would plummet. It would destroy the entire company if this got out."

"It's never gonna get out, kid. Relax."

"Fuck you, relax!"

James threw his glass over the balcony. In less than a second, he had Raj by the throat and was pressing him against the railing.

"I did what I thought was best, you little prick. I built this company with my sweat and my blood, and I'll be damned if some elephant-worshipping pissant is gonna tell me what to do."

Raj pushed back, but he was no match for James's wiry strength. He began slipping backward, his feet coming off the balcony.

"Let him go, Bill," Milton said calmly. "We have enough to deal with."

James let go, and Raj collapsed, gasping for air. He looked up at James with venom in his eyes as he got to his feet.

"I quit," Raj said.

As Raj stormed out, James leaned against the railing and folded his arms, gazing down at the imported carpet that covered the balcony floor. "We really fucked this. Real good this time."

Milton shrugged. "You did what you thought was best. That's what leaders do."

"Cal's goin' to the Feds. I know the whiny prick, and he's gonna go straight to the Feds."

"With what? A story about how some Russian broke into his house and he must've been sent by you? Where's the evidence?"

"Not that. He's got everything else."

"What else does he know?"

"We've been pumping our stock up since before I hired you. Cal knows where the right documents are and who to ask the right questions to. It's all fake, Milton. All of it. It's pumped with naked short-selling, rumor mills, accountants I got on the payroll... this company's going bankrupt. It would've been bankrupt a long time ago if it wasn't for me. That's why this Cuba deal is so important. It's our last shot."

Milton finished his drink and placed the glass down on the floor. "Well, then, there's only one option that I see."

"What's that?"

"Let's go to the Feds first. They tend to give immunity to whoever cooperates first. We'll... adjust the paper trail and point the fingers at Raj and Cal. We'll claim ignorance."

James sighed. "I'd rather kill him than turn him in. I'm a lotta things, but a rat ain't one of them."

"You can have your integrity and sit in a prison cell the rest of your life, or you can retire to a beach house in Florida and give testimony for two weeks at a trial. It's your choice."

He rubbed the bridge of his nose, feeling the first twinges of a painful migraine coming on. "Fucking business. You know where it all went wrong? We got the government involved. Gaming commission, regulatory committee, treasury department... it's too much. It's strangling us."

Milton stood up and slipped on his shoes. "Strangled or not, we need to go to the Feds first. We've lost control of this thing, Bill. It's time to fold."

As Milton left, James turned back to the city. He used to look at the lights, the naked women, and the glittering casino floors and see his city. It was an extension of himself. As he lived and breathed, so did the casinos. If the lights were to go out and the glitter turn to dust, he felt as if his heart would stop, and he would turn to dust as well.

He knew he couldn't be a rat, no matter what the prize was. Loyalty was ingrained in him. Back on the streets, when he was a kid, making one dollar here and five dollars there, the performers all knew there was a bond holding them together. If one street kid got busted, the others could count on him to never tell the cops anything. They were starving, broke, and hustling just to eat one candy bar a day, but they had their code.

James finished his drink and placed the glass down on a side table. He took off his watch and placed it down softly next to the glass. He walked to the railing, climbed over it, and looked down at the people below. He thought about the headlines the next day—"Casino Mogul Takes Out Six People on Sidewalk"— and it made him laugh. He felt warm tears on his cheeks and he looked up at the stars, which were hardly visible. The lights from the city drowned them.

He took a deep breath and climbed back to his balcony before going inside to make another drink. There were times he felt absolutely drained, like a spent battery. Many people—including

VICTOR METHOS

Hemingway, whom James had known for a time in the '50s—believed nature was where a man renewed himself. That had never worked for James. He thought of nature as a necessary evil. Where other men saw a mountain, he saw mining operations. Where they saw forests and fresh air, he saw condominiums and strip malls. There was only one place he could go and feel the electricity of youth pump through him. He finished his drink then headed down to the casino floor.

37

It was nearly midnight and Stanton was lying on his side, staring out the windows at the strip. The rumbling of the volcano display started every so often, and the deep bass of the drums pounded in his head. He sat up, knowing sleep was impossible for the night, and fumbled in a few of the drawers on the dresser before finding a packet of Advil liquid gels. He took two with a few swigs of orange juice and dressed before heading out the door.

The hallway was empty and the colors swirled before him. The multitude of designs, shapes, and hues of reds, oranges and blues disoriented him, and he stared at the floor as he made his way to the elevator. A man in a bathrobe stood in front of the vending machines, holding a full bucket of ice. He was swearing and pushing the machine.

"Excuse me," he said, "you don't have change for a twenty, do you? The machine ate my last dollar."

"Let me check." Stanton pulled out his wallet. He had three dollar bills, which he gave to the man.

"Well, just owe me the rest, I guess."

"No, it's fine," Stanton said, refusing to take the twenty.

"You sure?"

"Yeah."

"Thanks."

Stanton went to the elevators and pushed the down button. The man yelled, "Damn it!"

He looked over and saw that the man's next choice, a Twix bar, was stuck.

"My luck this trip," the man said. "Lost six grand at the tables and five bucks in this machine." He tried rocking it back and forth then began pounding on the glass.

Stanton walked over. "Let me try." He reached under the flap where the items were dispensed and quickly withdrew his hand, letting the flap snap shut. The Twix bar tipped. He did it again, and it fell.

"Hey, how'd you do that?"

"It's a closed system, so the air created from that motion shoots up the machine and then back down."

"Wow. I'll have to remember that. Thanks."

"No problem."

Stanton went toward the elevators again.

"Wait a second. What's your name?"

"Jon."

"Jon, I'm Jason. Nice to meet you."

"You as well."

"Hey, what're you doing tonight?"

"I was... well, nothing really."

"Why don't you come back to my room? I got a suite, biggest one on the floor."

"It's all right, thank you."

"Now don't be hasty. This isn't an invitation I make that often. But I got my wife back there, and I think it'd be a blast if we had some fun together."

Stanton didn't respond. The elevator dinged and opened, and he stepped on.

As the doors closed, the man said, "Your loss."

He leaned back against the mirrors lining the elevator and closed his eyes. One of the passages in Genesis had always resonated with him, even as a child:

Then the Lord rained down upon Sodom and Gomorrah brimstone and fire from the Lord out of Heaven. And he overthrew those cities, and all the plain, and all the inhabitants of the cities, and that which grew upon the ground.

The last phrase was what had stuck with him. As a child, he'd imagined God sitting on a cloud, overcome with anger at the evil he saw in these cities, casting down fire and brimstone and causing earthquakes and floods. Filled with so much rage that his creation would disobey him, he destroyed everything that lived, even the grass and the trees. It had filled Stanton with terror. As he grew older, he no longer feared that image. Instead, he feared what had occurred in Sodom and Gomorrah. Good men, he knew, were only one decision away from becoming evil men.

The elevator came to a stop at the lobby and he stepped out and went to the casino floor, which was crowded with drunken gamblers. Some were in evening wear, rolling dice, and others were chain-smoking at the three-card poker tables. The slot machines rang and rang, drowning out the sound of the Doors' "L.A. Woman" that was playing over the speakers. Cocktail waitresses were moving at a feverish pace, getting as many drinks as possible into the crowd. They were rewarded with dollar chips.

Stanton left and walked the strip for what seemed like a long time. He came to the Havana and stood outside, staring up at the lights shooting into space. He made his way inside and went to the casino. It looked no different from the one he was just in.

Stanton walked around the edge of the floor, one hand in his pocket and the other running lightly along the smooth walls. The display of shining steel running along the ceiling in that area was made to look like a river flowing upside down. Stanton stopped and watched it for a long time before moving on. He eventually made his way to a lounge that had funky furniture from the '60s. The area was as crowded as the rest of the casino, and small groups of people were relaxing and enjoying fruity cocktails as they flirted and laughed. Stanton noticed a tall figure leaning against the wall, slowly sucking on a cigarette. He was about to walk past him when he heard one of the pit bosses walk by and say, "Evening, Mr. James."

Stanton stopped. He was sufficiently far away, and there were enough people around that Stanton thought Bill James wouldn't notice him. He watched the other man. His simple movements were elegant. The way he lifted his arm and placed the cigarette between his lips, the softness of his exhalations as the smoke left his nostrils, and the way he crossed one foot over the other gave Stanton the impression of a 1930s leading man. He seemed to be from a different generation, one that was nearly gone.

James stood under a flashing sign that said, "Visit us anytime. We never sleep."

38

Alma Parr waited until the sun broke over the horizon before he slipped on the Kevlar vest and his sunglasses. The three other people in the car began prepping, too. He checked his sidearm then placed it back in the holster. The SWAT van was twenty feet away to the west. A few of the men were stretching and taking nervous pisses. Back when he was in SWAT, he had to crap before every raid.

Behind the van sat two men in ankle and wrist cuffs, with two SWAT officers behind them holding semi-automatic rifles. The men were staring at the ground. One of them was having minor convulsions and tremors. It had been a while since his last hit.

"How'd you know they'd have sentries?" Javier asked from the backseat.

"Because I'm paranoid, and that's what I would do if I ran a compound." Parr took a deep breath. "Sun's up. Let's go."

He slipped out of the car and left the door open. Aside from the SWAT van, at least half a dozen cruisers with uniforms were standing by. The SWAT commander, who was in the passenger seat of the van, looked over and gave the thumbs-up. Parr did the same and SWAT officers silently hopped out of the van and began making their way to the compound entrance, which wasn't more than thirty feet away.

Parr fiddled with the lock on the gate, hoping to break it off, but it was solid. He looked back at the SWAT commander and motioned for the van to break through the gate. The commander whispered to one of the officers next to him, and he ran back to the van and turned it on. Parr and his men scattered as the van roared down the dirt road and crashed into the gate, ripping it off its hinges. The officers swarmed in.

Two women were out smoking and they screamed. One of the officers grabbed them both by the back of the neck and threw them in the dirt. He put his boot on one of them and had his rifle turned on the other.

Parr had gotten the layout from one of the sentries. He had refused to cooperate, so Parr had asked for a few minutes alone with him in the back of the van. The other officers took a break, and it didn't take much for Parr to get what he needed.

Three of the five buildings were housing, but the last two had operational functions. One was the meeting place and housing for the leaders of this sector of the Brotherhood, which consisted of eleven men in total. The other was a heavily guarded weapons and drug cache armory.

SWAT went for the armory while Parr, Jay, Javier, and three officers went into the leadership's stronghold. Shots rang out from the various buildings, then the crackle of return fire filled the air. Parr kicked down the door and went in gun first. He swung left and right as the others came in behind him.

They were inside a bar. Rather than walking around them, Parr kicked over tables as he made his way through. The surprise had worn off, and now the guys had to feel intimidated. Otherwise, the officers were in for a fight.

A blast behind them threw Jay off his feet and over a table. Parr swung around and saw a man behind the bar lift his shotgun and aim at one of the other officers. Parr fired twice. The first shot went through the man's forearm and the shotgun fell to the floor. He held up his hands in surrender and screamed, "Don't shoot!" Parr fired again, sending a round through his eye, spattering skull and brain matter on the liquor bottles behind him.

Jay was choking and coughing as he pulled off the hot Kevlar. Parr bent over him and scanned his back. It was bruised with half-inch purple-and-black circles, but there was no blood.

"Stay here," Parr said.

"No fucking way."

Jay got to his feet and put the Kevlar back on, still coughing.

Parr told one of the other officers, "Stay behind him."

They made their way through the bar to the door at the far end. Parr took one side and Javier took the other. He could hear machine-gun fire outside, and the high-pitched squeal of pistols. Parr held up his hand, counting down. *Three, two, one...*

He kicked open the door to a large room with furniture, a computer, swastika posters and a Confederate flag. There was a bed in the room and the sheets had decorations of skulls on them. They walked through the room silently, watching the door on the other side. Parr glanced at the closet. He tried to blink away the hot sting of sweat in his eyes. He got to the closet and flung open the door.

A woman screamed, and he placed his weapon against her head. He lowered it when he saw that she wasn't armed. He grabbed her by the hair and threw her to the floor. There was no one else in the closet.

As he turned to go to the unopened door, three shots went off in succession. An officer screamed and tumbled to the floor, his ankle a mass of slick, wet, flesh and bone.

"Under the bed!" Javier shouted.

Parr jumped to the floor on his side as two more shots went off. The man under the bed looked up just as Parr pulled the trigger. His mouth opened to scream and the round went down his throat and out the back of his neck. He was choking and gurgling as Javier grabbed his feet and pulled him from under the bed. The woman was screaming frantically and it was hurting Parr's ears. He looked at the officer's ankle then at the woman. He lifted his firearm and slammed the handle across her head just behind the ear, knocking her out.

"Get him out."

Two officers helped the injured man limp out of the room as Parr went to the door. It led out to a hallway with three rooms on one side and two on the other. He thought about waiting for

SWAT to join him, but he could hear the firefight still raging in the next building.

He made a flurry of hand signals, directing two officers down one side of the hallway and two down the other. He and Javier took the right side. Parr slid along the wall, keeping low. He passed quickly by the first door, glancing in. It was an empty bathroom. He was about to turn away when he noticed the cupboards underneath the sink. He leaned down and opened them. A man was curled up tightly, his back to Parr.

Parr whispered, "I'm about to blow your brains over that Lysol bottle. You have one chance to live. Show me your hands and quietly climb out."

The man, shaking, showed his hands and began to slip out. Javier searched him and placed cuffs on him, pinning his hands behind his back.

They moved on to the next room. Parr glanced over at Jay and the other officer, who had just come out of a room across the hall. They shook their heads. Parr turned to the room in front of him and went inside. It was a child's bedroom. There were stuffed animals on the bed and toys strewn across the floor. Behind the dresser was a young girl, no more than twelve. Parr put his finger to his lips. "Shh," he said as he pulled her out.

She had been crying and he gently placed his hand on her shoulder. He leaned close and whispered, "I don't want to hurt anyone here. Tell me where your parents are so that more people don't have to get hurt."

"They're not my parents," she whispered back, anger in her voice.

Parr looked around the room. The closet was open. Lingerie hung on hangers, along with high heels meant for a child. Rage tingled down his spine.

"Wait here for me. I'll be right back."

"No, don't leave me." She grabbed his arm. "Please."

"Sweetie, I will be right back. You just sit here and wait for me."

She began to cry. "No, no please."

Parr looked at Javier. "Get her outta here."

"I'm not leaving you."

"Do it. Now."

Parr went into the hallway as Javier lifted the girl in his arms and headed back the way they'd come in. Jay and the officer came out of the last room on their side of the hall, shaking their heads. There was one room left and the door was closed.

Parr stood in front of the door, sweat rolling off his face and onto his arms and hands. He watched three drops trickle down. No sounds came from the room. He placed his hand on the knob, twisted, and pushed open the door.

Brody was sitting in a chair, smoking a joint. Three Rottweilers, thick chains around their collars, waited at his feet. Brody held the end of the chains in the same hand holding the joint. In the other hand was a 12-gauge shotgun.

"Mornin'." He flicked the joint onto the floor, and with it, the chains.

The dogs rushed forward. Parr lifted his weapon but teeth clamped down on his arm and twisted him to the side. Another dog bit into his thigh as Jay lifted his weapon. A thunderous boom ricocheted around the room as Brody's weapon tore Jay's leg in half and he fell to the floor screaming.

The terrified uniformed officer stepped back into the hall as Brody rose to his feet and fired another round. The third dog chased the officer, who got off one round, which went into the ceiling when the dog tore into his inner thigh.

Parr saw the massive amount of blood pouring out of him onto the hardwood floors. The Rottweiler on his arm twisted so hard that he flew into nearby boxes. The second dog had a death grip on his thigh and refused to let go. The dog on his arm released its grip and went for his throat.

Parr held up his forearm to block it and the dog ripped into it so violently that a spray of warm blood hit Parr's face like rain. It jerked its head back and forth, sliding Parr across the floor like a rag. He lifted his other hand and saw that his gun was gone. The dog on his thigh tried to pull him farther down and Parr jabbed his finger into its eye hard enough to pry it from its socket. Howling in pain, the dog released its grip.

Parr spotted his gun next to a closet door. He lunged for it just as the other dog leapt for his face again. He pulled up his gun and fired a round into the dog's brain. With a whimper, the lifeless body fell on top of him. He swung around, pressed the muzzle against the other dog's ear, and fired. It didn't let go. He fired again and again until the dog went limp, but it still didn't let go. He pried open its jaws and got to his feet. The burning pain of torn flesh rocketed through his leg. Brody was nowhere to be seen.

Parr limped to the wall and leaned against it, his gun near his face. He lowered his gun and went to the door, sliding against the wall because he was unable to walk without support. He peeked out. The uniformed officer was on his stomach, a large pool of blood around the gushing wound in his back. Muffled screams came from the room where he had left the girl.

Pushing one hand against the wall, he hobbled around to the door and glanced in, then quickly backed away. He'd seen Brody on the floor, the girl held between his arms, and a dog next to them. He hadn't seen Javier. Parr looked back in.

"Howdy," Brody said. His face was bright crimson, his eyes so red Parr thought they might have been bleeding.

"Let her go."

"Now why would I do that? Me and this little darlin' have had some fun times. Haven't we, Daisy?"

Parr stepped slowly into the room.

"I wouldn't do that if I were you," Brody said. "One word and my pup'll rip out her throat. Or maybe I'll just blow her head clean off and dirty that nice dress'a hers."

Parr could see the shotgun lying next to Brody. Both his hands were on the girl.

"The gunfire's stopped," Parr said. "You've lost. Let her go."

"Why you all come here anyway? We didn't do nothin'. We just wanted to be left alone."

"You didn't do nothin'? What about her?"

"You didn't know about her when you came. No one did. This here's a little Southern peach we picked up in Louisiana. No way you knew about her."

"Freddy Steed."

He laughed. "All this bullshit over a queer like Freddy Steed? Fuck Freddy Steed."

"You killed him."

"Hell yes I killed him. I can't have no fudge-packers in my city. That other queer, Tyler—that queer's gonna get what's comin' to him, too. I can tell you that."

"They were lovers?"

"They weren't lovers," he said angrily. "Queers can't be lovers. They can just be queers."

"Well you'll find out soon enough in the can."

He smirked. "I ain't goin' nowhere. I can't live in a cage."

Parr looked at the dog then down at the shotgun. Brody moved behind the girl, shielding most of his body with hers. For a moment, neither of them moved or even breathed. They existed in that moment separately, but they knew it was the last moment of one of their lives, and they shared something. It was brief, like a flash of heat that comes and goes, but Parr recognized it. He closed his eyes, just for a fraction of second, and as he opened them, the gun came up.

Brody released the girl and the dog lunged for her. Parr fired right through the dog's throat, and it collapsed into a heap of growling pain, blood and wet fur. The blast from the shotgun struck Parr like a truck and he flew backward, off his feet, and hit the wall in the hallway. He slid down to the floor and as he did so, he fired his last three rounds as Brody got to his feet with his shotgun at his shoulder for better aim.

Suddenly, Brody lowered the gun. He looked at Parr, a smile on his face, and blood began to leak from the small hole in his forehead. Then blood sprayed out in time with the beating of his heart in such enormous quantities that it soaked the girl at his feet, dying her clothes a dark red, sticking her hair to her head.

Parr got to his knees as she huddled on the floor, in shock. Boots stomped up the hall as Parr ripped the smoking vest off his chest and wrapped his arms around the crying girl.

39

Stanton sat across from Mindi in the booth at the café while she recounted what she had heard that morning regarding the raid on the compound. He twisted an Equal packet in his hands as he listened, picturing the space littered with empty shells and bodies. Nine members of the Brotherhood and two officers were dead. They had found a weapons cache unlike anything they could have dreamed. From grenades to rocket launchers to sniper rifles, the Brotherhood had been preparing for war. It had also turned up one of the largest stashes of methamphetamine in Nevada's history. Two young girls who had been kidnapped from different parts of the country had also been found.

The story of the hero cops who'd freed two captive children was all over the Internet and in all the papers. A photo of Alma Parr being taken out of an ambulance and into an emergency room was featured prominently in every story. There were also two of Orson Hall standing next to a mountain of weapons and methamphetamine wrapped in thick plastic bricks.

"I can't believe I missed that," Mindi said. "I shoulda been there for them. Oh, by the way, I talked to Alma in the hospital. He doesn't think you did anything to Freddy. You're in the clear."

"Is he doing all right?"

"Yeah, he's going to be okay. He's one of the toughest guys I've ever known."

"Did they find anything related to the Steeds?"

"No. Why? Do you think Brody did that?"

"They killed Freddy. It wouldn't be a stretch to think they killed his parents, too. I was hoping they might find something."

"Not that I know of, but I wasn't there. I can go talk to Orson about it. He's been there all day."

"It wouldn't hurt."

"What're you going to be doing?"

"I need to go to the Flamingo."

"Why?"

"That's the last place I asked Marty to go. I need to see if he actually went. Maybe someone there saw something." He finished his glass of orange juice and wiped his lips before leaving cash on the table. "Call me if Orson knows anything."

"I will."

Stanton walked out of the café and to the car he had rented that morning. It was an old Toyota, not much more than four wheels and a frame, but it was cheap and safe. He glanced back at the café and saw Mindi mulling something over, absent-mindedly nibbling at her food. There was something between them, but acting on it was a different matter. He got the impression that she would never leave the force for any man and he didn't have plans to live in Las Vegas. Stanton wondered if a normal man would have thought about dating and having fun rather than a long-term relationship.

He parked at a meter outside the precinct then went to reception and asked for Detective Stewart in Narcotics. The receptionist told him to hold on and buzzed the detective. Stanton waited in the lobby, where a couple of the officers recognized him and murmured under their breath. Ignoring them, he picked up a *Time* magazine. The person of the year was "The Protestor;" a person whose face was hidden behind a scarf graced the cover. He threw the magazine back down without opening it and leaned back in the chair.

Before long, a detective with a thick mustache came out. He had white, hairy forearms exposed by a short-sleeved button-down shirt.

"Mr. Stanton," he said in a thick voice, "I'm Ian Stewart. What can I do for you?"

Stanton stood up. "I have a message from Brody." He took out the slip of paper and handed it to him.

"What is this?"

"The date and time of a large shipment of cocaine."

Steward folded the slip of paper and put it in his pocket. "Brody's dead, you know."

"I know, but I promised him I would do this. I keep my promises."

Stewart nodded and glanced around to see if anybody was within earshot. "It's a shame, actually. He was a good soldier in the war against the mud people."

Stanton was so caught off guard by the comment that he didn't respond. He just turned and walked away.

"What? You think you're better than me?" Stewart asked. "'Cause you stand by while they take over our country and I actually want to do something about it?"

Stanton turned back to him. "Whatever you put into the world is what you get back. All that hatred and fear, one day it's going to come to your house to collect."

Stanton checked his watch. It was nearly five p.m. He had been sitting in his car for over an hour, watching the security guard at the Hilton Vacation Suites-Flamingo front desk, a man in his mid-sixties just waiting for retirement. He spent most of his time surfing the Internet or reading magazines. He fell asleep for a little while, then someone with a question woke him. This wasn't a man who would be impressed by the badge or go out of his way to help anyone in need. His primary motivation was laziness.

Stanton got out of the car and went inside. Soft music was playing over the speakers, and a family brushed past him to get outside.

The young boy whined, "But I don't want to go there!"

The parents didn't respond and when he protested by trying to sit down, the father dragged him by his arm until he started walking again.

Stanton stood at the desk and glanced at the computer screen that the guard was glued to. The net browser was open to a sportsman's website, which discussed the benefits of bow hunting versus rifle.

"Hi," Stanton said.

"What can I do for ya?" he said without looking up.

Stanton took out his badge and held it within the guard's field of vision. The guard looked up at him but didn't read the badge. Stanton replaced it in his pocket.

"A colleague of mine might have come by here in the last ten days or so." He took out his cell phone and brought up the photo Mindi had emailed him. "Do you recognize him?"

The guard looked at the photo of Marty. "Nope."

"You sure?"

"Yup," he said, turning back to his computer screen.

"That's too bad. This officer was murdered recently. I'm going to need you to come down to the station with me."

"For what?"

"I think you were one of the last people to see him alive, so we need to go through the tapes from the lobby together."

"I ain't goin' anywhere."

"You can come with me voluntarily or I can arrest you for obstruction."

"Obstruction! What you talkin' about? I ain't done nothin'."

"You're hampering the murder investigation of a police officer. It won't take more than a day or two. We'll have some forms for you, too, but a lot of those can be filled out at home. I'll clear it with your boss."

The man grew flustered, his lips trembling. "I ain't done nothin'."

"Then was he here or not?"

"Yeah, yeah, he was here. Some... I don't know, five or six days ago."

"What did he ask you?"

"He asked for a tape. Um, some tape from the camera near the tram."

"Did you give it to him?"

"Yeah, I gave it to him."

"Do you have a copy of that tape?"

"No, it was on a disc, like a DVD, and we just throw 'em away after a few weeks. We don't keep copies."

"Was anyone with this man when he came to see you?"

"No... no, he was alone." The guard thought a second. "But he got a call. Yeah, I remember that. He got a call from someone and told them he had a tape that they thought ... I don't remember exactly what he said, but somethin' about having caught something on tape."

"Did he mention the name of the caller?"

"No, the guy seemed kinda slow so I didn't ask no questions. I just gave him the disc and he signed for it and left."

Stanton tapped the counter. "Thanks."

"Hey, wait a second. Is that it? I don't need to come down and fill out no papers or nothin', right?"

Stanton walked out without responding. He dialed Mindi. The call went to voicemail and he said, "Call me back right away. I know what he was looking for inside Marty's house."

40

Prickly excitement in his belly, Stanton sped down the free-way to Marty's house. He suddenly realized he hadn't had any-thing to eat or drink since that morning. He felt lightheaded and a headache was coming on. He pulled off the freeway into a bur-ger joint and went inside, where he ordered a vegetarian burger and a Diet Coke with fries. It took all his willpower to simply place his order and sit at a table rather than run out to his car and get back on the freeway. He ate slowly so he wouldn't upset his stomach and stared out the window at the passing traffic. Watching groups of people made him uncomfortable. It hadn't always. When he was a kid and his mother had taken him to the mall or Disneyland, the groups had excited him, but ever since he'd joined the force, his thoughts always drifted to unpleasant things. How many of the men out there beat their wives? Or how many were drunk and would kill somebody on the road? How many of them were planning a home invasion? How many of them thought about these things but didn't act on them?

"Are you done, sir?"

Stanton snapped back to where he was and what he was doing, realizing the young busser cleaning tables had spoken to him. "Yeah, thanks."

He took his Diet Coke with him and headed back to his car. He caught a glimpse of his eyes in the rearview mirror and it made him pause. His son, Mathew, had the same eyes. An intense ache gripped his chest and he had the urge to drive back to San Diego and take his kids in his arms. But the draw of Marty's house was too strong. It was a magnet and he was a piece of steel, sliding toward it on a smooth surface.

The freeway drive was pleasant. He rolled down his window and let the evening air fill the car. The light scent of smoke mingled with the warm night air. The fire was somewhere off in the distance, far enough away that the smell was pleasant.

He turned off the freeway and found Flower Avenue. He counted the homes until he came to the fifth one down where he parked in the driveway. He was glad for the streetlamp behind him, illuminating the sidewalk and part of the driveway. He got out of the car and shut the door. Then he leaned against it for a moment, listening to the neighborhood. A television was on in the house next door, some sitcom with canned laughter. The blue flicker of the screen illuminated the curtains and he could see a man sitting in his boxer shorts sipping on a tall can of beer.

His heart pounding, Stanton walked up the driveway. He had been kidnapped the last time he was there, and the full impact of it hadn't settled yet. He was able to disassociate experiences in his mind and keep going. The kidnapping was an experience to be analyzed and dissected and to draw conclusions from. If he treated it like an intellectual exercise, it didn't bother him. It didn't have the impact on him that it would have had on someone who wasn't used to seeing what he saw every day.

At the front door, the doorknob was unlocked but the deadbolt wasn't. He went around back, checking the windows. The backyard was dark and he took out a penlight he had on his keychain and flashed it on the backdoor. It was locked as well. The basement window hadn't been replaced yet, but the broken glass had been cleared away. Taking a deep breath, he climbed down and went inside.

Inside the house, he paused. He put the penlight between his teeth, took out his firearm, and held it low. The weight of it, the smooth steel of the trigger, and the rough edges of the barrel against his thigh were like slipping into a well-worn silk shirt that fell over his shoulders like water. It was familiar and warm.

It calmed him, allowing him to focus. He could see why egotists chose law enforcement more often than any other profession. There was a sense of power in being allowed to carry and take out a gun wherever one wanted.

Upstairs, he came to the three doors he had been to before and chose the one on the right. It was a sparsely decorated bedroom with little more than a bed and a painting on the wall. The house was still and silent, so quiet that he could hear the crickets outside.

Marty was dead two days before we found him. You had two days in here by yourself.

He slid open a closet. He reached down, brushing aside some clothing.

Two days and you didn't find anything. You tried to stay so neat. You didn't want anyone to know that you were here but you couldn't clean everything. I interrupted you before you put the cushions back and cleaned up the drawers. You had to leave those out.

After closing the closet, Stanton checked under the bed. He stood up again and looked around. He went back to the hall and opened the other door, which opened into a storage closet. He began going through the shelves.

You must've gone crazy looking through here. You wished you hadn't killed Marty. He could've told you where it was and now you're stuck. But you couldn't spend the whole two days here, either. You had other things to do. People would notice you were gone. When you were doing other things, your mind was still here. This was all you could think about.

The storage closet was packed with two feet of junk. Marty had clearly filled it with everything that had nowhere else to go. It would take Stanton all night to search through it. He stepped back out into the basement and stood in the center of the room. He closed his eyes, listening to the sounds of the house as it settled for the night.

You were so meticulous. You thought you were checking everywhere you could check, but you couldn't find it. Marty hid it too well. He watched the disc. He saw what was on it. It was your face, and he knew who you were. That's the only reason he would take this much effort to hide it. He knew you, and he knew you would come after him. But if you couldn't find it in two days, I won't either. The house is too big. There's too much to go through. Unless it's...

He opened his eyes and turned, looking out the window at the backyard.

Unless it's not in the house.

He climbed out and stood in the large backyard. The quickest and most effective way to search a large space was with constricting circles. Stanton started at the edge of the fence and worked his way around, the penlight pointed at the ground. He took off his shoes to feel for any bumps or displaced dirt or grass.

He finished the first circle then continued with the second, the third and the fourth. Somewhere near the center of the yard his foot hit a small indentation. He stepped on it again, gingerly, so as not to disturb it too much. He knelt and put the penlight over it. There was a small bump in the lawn. Someone had cut a square into the grass, placed something underneath, then put the grass back over it. He lifted the sod and underneath was a plastic case. Stanton wished he had thought to bring latex gloves.

He opened the case, making sure only to touch the edges. The disc inside was labeled June 12.

41

Mindi Tiffany Morgan sat in the police cruiser. She was in the backseat, a uniform was driving, and Orson Hall was in the passenger seat. She stared out the window at the passing desert. She'd spent hours at that compound and found nothing linking it to the Steeds' murder. Of course, she wasn't a detective, but she was smart. She had earned a 4.0 in criminal justice with an emphasis in forensics. She would be a detective one day. But right now, she didn't have that edge. Most of the detectives she knew—at least the serious crimes detectives, like the ones in Homicide and Sex Crimes—had something that other officers either didn't have or hadn't fully developed yet: an ability to make connections that normal people couldn't. At the compound she'd tried desperately to make those connections from what she saw around her, but it was no use. To her, every scene was just a bunch of junk.

Her cell phone rang.

Orson glanced back and asked, "Who is it?"

"It's Jon." She answered the call. "Hey... no way! Where?... no, there's a law enforcement media player called Integra. It's probably coded on that. I have it on my home computer. Meet me at my house... no, I'll text you the address. How long will you be?... okay... Orson's giving me a ride home... all right. Bye."

"What did he want?" Orson said.

"He found something at Marty's house."

"What?"

"A disc."

He turned and faced her. "Mindi, he's not a police officer here. He can't go around to crime scenes on his own and mess with things. What if we find out who did this and it goes to court? A defense attorney would have a field day with that tidbit."

"Nobody else could find it, Orson. CSI went through that place with a microscope."

He shook his head and turned back around. "You meeting him at your house?"

"Yeah, do you mind dropping me off?"

"No, that's fine." He shifted in his seat and laid his head back on the headrest. "So, you and Jon, you guys…"

"No."

"Oh, sorry. I just figured 'cause of how much you talk about him. He's a good-looking guy."

"I know. It's not that I wouldn't. He's just a lot different from the guys I've dated. I think he needs me to be the one to ask."

"His ex, Melissa, was a lot like you. We went on a few vacations together. She was a spitfire, never taking shit from anybody. Jon seems to attract strong women."

The drive was long and Mindi grew restless. She surfed the Internet on her phone, read through a few articles in the *New York Times* and *Vanity Fair*, and stared out the window at the endless expanse of desert. Under the night sky it appeared little more than black with tall shadowy peaks breaking up the horizon.

Her house was located in a quiet suburb not far from the Strip. A long driveway led to a two-car garage and a decent-sized lawn. By the time the police cruiser came to a stop in the driveway she was asleep. Orson reached back and shook her leg. She woke up, thanked them for the ride, and went inside her home. She glanced back and saw Orson wave at her.

Stanton held the disc and carefully avoided getting fingerprints on it. He tucked it into his jacket as he got into his car and typed Mindi's address into Google Maps. It was forty-one minutes away.

The drive was brisk and he drove down Las Vegas Boulevard at the height of the evening, before everyone had gotten drunk, had sex, or lost all their money at the tables. Exhilaration still tickled the air.

He didn't notice the lights or the people. He kept lightly touching the disc in his pocket, eager to see the video that would put a face to the man he was after. The man had been nothing more than a shadow, an outline of a person. Now he would have an identity, parents, possibly a wife and kids, neighbors and friends. He was a real person, not a demon. That was usually the most difficult part of Stanton's job, and he never grew used to recognizing what normal people were capable of doing to each other... and that they enjoyed it.

He parked on the curb outside her house. A police cruiser was in the driveway. He figured Orson must have stayed, which was good. If Marty knew the person on the disc the odds were that Orson knew him as well.

Stanton walked up the lawn, glancing once at the crescent moon, and knocked on the door. Mindi shouted to come in; he opened the door and stepped inside.

Mindi was on her knees against the wall in front of him in the living room. She was staring down at the carpet; the fear and anger on her face spoke to him as loudly as a scream would have. About five feet to her side was an officer in uniform. He was lying on his back and blood trickled from a wound in his head. Stanton went to check on him, but a voice stopped him.

"Glad you came, Jon." Orson was sitting on the sofa, a revolver pointed at Stanton's chest. "Please, have a seat."

42

Stanton froze next to the door. He felt the breeze on his back. A couple of steps backward would take him out of the house. He could easily run down the street and place a call. He looked at Mindi, who was trembling.

"Shut the door please, Jon."

Stanton didn't move for a full half minute, and Orson didn't repeat what he had said. Instead, Stanton lowered his hand near his firearm.

"Jon, please don't be stupid. If you run I'm going to shoot her in the head. Then I'll shoot myself in the shoulder, throw the gun outside somewhere, and say it was you. Forensics will eventually prove me wrong, but I'll be long gone by then. They'll arrest you first. You know that. Now please, shut the door and sit down."

Stanton took a deep breath and closed the door.

"Now lock it."

He twisted the deadbolt and turned to face Orson. Stanton didn't drop his holster, and wouldn't if he was asked to.

"Oh, man," Orson said, "things went bad on this. Real bad. People I didn't want to get hurt ended up getting hurt."

"Kill me and let her go, Orson. Tie her up and leave her here and hop on a plane. Go to South America and they'll never find you."

"Yeah, probably. I got a lot to lose here, though. I got a house, a pension, assets. I got power here. How can I go from that to living in some shack in Belize?"

"It's better than a needle."

He exhaled loudly. "Man, I shoulda killed you in that basement when I had the chance. You have this fucking ability to get into people's heads, don't you? That's probably why Melissa left you. You drove her crazy."

"Why did you bring me out here, Orson? Was it only to try and blame me for all this?"

"I couldn't blame one of my own. But an outsider? Hell, no one would give a shit about some academic from San Diego, especially one with a past like yours." He laughed. "I told everyone that you're psychic, Jon. I was bullshitting them, but now... I don't know. Are you psychic? I mean you're definitely a freak, but can you actually see things other people can't?"

Headlights shone into the house as a car pulled up next to the cruiser in the driveway.

"Good, he's here. Mindi," Orson said, "unlock the door, please."

She unlocked the door then hesitated for an instant as she looked outside through the open door. Orson cocked his revolver and she went back to her spot by the wall.

Bill James entered, wearing an Armani suit with no tie. He looked at Mindi then at the officer on the ground. Then he saw Stanton standing in front of Orson. His eyes drifted to the gun.

"What the hell are you doing? You wanna get the fucking death penalty?"

Orson chuckled. "You forget the word 'we' pretty quickly, don't you, Bill?"

"Fuck your 'we.' Who told you to rape Emily Steed? You could have shot 'em both when they were getting into their car and no one would have seen a damn thing."

Stanton looked at Orson. "How much did he pay you?"

"A lot. But believe it or not, Jon, I went to him." Orson's face contorted briefly into a slight sneer on his lips that quickly disappeared. "I loved her, man. I was gonna leave Wendy for her. I ain't kiddin'. My kids woulda never forgiven me, but I didn't care. She was the one—the one I wanted to grow old with. When I told her that, you know what she said to me, Jon? She laughed. She just fucking laughed right in my face. She said I wasn't in her class, that it was fun but her pool boy was as good a fuck as I was and she wouldn't marry her pool boy." Tears streamed down his face, and he wiped them with the back of his sleeve. He laughed hysterically. "But, man, she got fucked in the end, didn't she?"

"You stupid son of a bitch," James said. "You gonna kill three police officers? They will never rest until they find out who did this. Never. They will fly every damn fed out here from Quantico until they find us. You think I wanna look over my shoulder for the rest of my life?"

"You're wrong about something there, Bill. I'm not gonna kill three cops. I'm gonna kill three cops and a casino owner."

James didn't move. Then, in a motion as quick and smooth as a gunslinger's, he pulled out his Smith & Wesson .40 and pointed it at Orson's head. "Put the fucking gun down."

A voice bellowed from behind them. "Both you cocksuckers put 'em down."

Alma Parr stood at the entrance to the kitchen. He was leaning on a cane, his weapon pointed at James' head.

As Orson glared at Parr, Stanton quickly stepped back and pulled out his firearm. He fell into the Weaver stance, fixing his weapon firmly on Orson's chest.

Orson laughed. "You gotta be shittin' me." He called out to Mindi, "Hey, honey, you got a gun, too? Maybe you can join us?"

James glanced from Parr to Stanton. "This isn't a good situation," he said nervously. "This has the potential to go real bad real fast unless we all calm down and take a breath."

"Take all the breaths you want," Parr said, "I ain't movin' this fucking gun."

Stanton said, "There's no need for anyone else to die. Orson, it's over. Drop your weapon."

"No way."

"You killed innocent people. It's gone too far. You have to go down."

"Innocent?" he said incredulously. "Daniel Steed threw poor people out on the street just to make a few extra bucks. His wife fucked everything with a dick whether it was married or not. How the hell are they innocent?"

"What about Freddy Steed? You had him burned to death for nothing."

"No, not nothing. I wanted Emily to feel what it was like to get your heart broken. Don't matter, though. He was a piece'a shit Nazi. A *Nazi*, Jon. Are you really trying to make me feel bad for taking him down?"

"He was a kid. He was barely old enough to drink. He deserved a chance to make his life straight."

He leaned forward, not taking the gun off Stanton. "You know, I am so sick of your bullshit. You really think there's a God? Huh? And he cares about us and makes sure we're doin' okay and gives us our bottles at night and tucks us in? I had Freddy Steed burned for fifteen hundred bucks. Fifteen hundred dollars, Jon. That's what it cost to snuff out a life. Where was your God then? He wasn't powerful enough to put out those flames."

"It's not like that. We have agency, Orson. We get to choose. We choose who we are. I know you. I know this isn't you. You can choose something different. Put your gun down. Turn yourself in. It's the only way."

Orson, fresh tears streaming down his face, sat up straight. He took a few breaths. "You believe in the devil, too, Jon? I don't mean a force of evil or anything like that. I mean an actual devil who whispers in your ear and tries to get you to do bad things?"

"Yes."

"Well, I'll tell him hello for you."

"Orson, no!"

Orson lifted the weapon to fire at Stanton. James fired first, followed by the loud pop of Parr firing before Stanton got off two rounds, hitting Orson in the chest. James took a hit to the back of the head and collapsed. Orson fell against the couch, twisted around, and fired three rounds at Parr, hitting him twice. He toppled over.

Stanton stood with his weapon out, still in his stance. His hearing was muffled. He had temporarily been deafened, but he could hear Mindi screaming. He felt an intense warmth that made him feel relaxed. He glanced down and saw the blood flowing from a wound in his stomach. He heard the last gurgled breath of Orson Hall, then he fell to his knees, lifted his head, and dropped to his side.

43

Mindi Morgan sat in the hospital waiting room at the Sunrise Medical Center for two days. She ate frequently at the cafeteria, although she was rarely hungry. She had been given a blanket and a pillow. She'd stretched out on several chairs to rest during the day. At night, the hospital staff brought her a cot to sleep on. In the middle of the night on both nights, she woke with a start. The second night it was accompanied by a scream, and one of the nurses came over to check if she was okay.

On the third day, a doctor, a young woman with reddish-brown hair and brown eyes, came to her and put a hand on her shoulder while Mindi stared absently at the television on the wall.

"Ms. Morgan?"

She looked at her, startled. "Yes?"

"Well, I think you'll be able to go home tonight. Mr. Stanton is doing very well. Our main worry was infection, but he seems to have fought that off. Would you like to see him?"

"Yes."

"Okay, I'll have a member of the staff come and get you. We only allow one visitor at a time."

"Thanks."

Mindi watched commercials as she waited. She contemplated going to the bathroom to freshen up but decided against it. She didn't want to miss her chance to visit Jon. Instead, she took a hair elastic from her purse and pulled her hair back. She took a few tissues from the box on the table next to her, dabbed some water on them from a bottle, and wiped her face clean.

"Mindi," the nurse said, "he's ready for you."

She followed the nurse down the corridor. It was large, white, and empty.

The nurse opened the door to room 202 and stepped inside. "You have a visitor eager to see you."

Stanton was lying on his back in the hospital bed. He had dark circles under his eyes and two IVs in his left arm. A man in a suit, holding a couple of thick black books, stood in front of the bed. He was smiling as he said, "It was very nice to meet you, Brother Stanton. Next time you come to Vegas, please stop by the congregation for service."

The man left, nodding hello to Mindi. She went closer to the bed and placed her hand over his. They stood quietly as the nurse straightened a few things. When she left, Mindi sat on a stool by the bed.

"I keep thinking about it." she said. "All the blood. The sounds. I can't get it out of my head."

"You will. Time'll push it out and eventually it won't even seem real anymore. You'll start asking yourself if it really happened." He shifted a little to the side, a grimace contorting his face. "How's Alma?"

"Both bullets went into his bicep and out the back of his arm. He's going to be okay. He said he wanted to come visit you as soon as you were better."

Stanton hesitated, feeling the cloth of his bed sheets between his fingers. "How did Alma know to come to your house, Mindi?"

She didn't say anything.

"I figured that's what it was. How long were you wired?"

"They told me I didn't have a choice. I could do it, or I could go write traffic tickets the rest of my career. I'm so sorry, Jon. It was a mistake. I understand if you don't want to see me anymore."

"No. If I turned away everyone I knew who made mistakes, I wouldn't have anybody left."

She gripped his hand tighter. "What are you going to do now?"

"I'd like to visit Orson's family. I want to talk to his kids but I think they'll hate me. I don't know if they would understand what happened. They're going to have a hard life ahead of them now. Everyone is going to tell them their father was a monster. I want to tell them that he had good qualities and he loved them very much."

"Well you can worry about that later. For now, you just work on getting better." She leaned down and kissed his lips. "I'm going to go home and take a shower."

"I wasn't going to say anything."

She chuckled. "I stink, don't I?"

"Little bit."

She kissed him again then left the room.

EPILOGUE

Stanton sat on his surfboard, letting the waves lap against his legs. The water was warm and he wished he didn't have to wear a wetsuit. He enjoyed the sensation of water against his skin.

He waited for his set and caught a good wave that rocketed him back to shore. He hopped up on the board and cut across the wave before spinning back around to go the other way. He had to crouch to get under the wave, and eventually it swallowed him. His world spun and his ears filled with the sound of rushing water and the heartbeat of the ocean. The ocean was alive. It fed, nurtured, reproduced and could die if it wasn't looked after.

He didn't move at first. He was facedown, looking at the clear blue water below him. He wondered how far down he could swim before his lungs burned and he was forced to come back up. He had the sudden urge to dive down and put his feet in the sand at the bottom, to bury them and walk along the bottom of the ocean just to see what was there.

He popped back up to the surface, taking a large gulp of air, and found his board. He got on and paddled back to shore.

Ocean Beach Park was his favorite place to surf in all of San Diego. The locals weren't rude, but they disliked outsiders just enough that few novices wanted to surf there. It wasn't a difficult beach, and the waves were always manageable, but there was something about the enjoyment of surfing that correlated directly to how many people were out there. Surfing was meant to be enjoyed alone, as a time to re-establish a connection with nature that people lost as they grew older and more civilized.

Stanton found his beach towel and lay down, feeling the hot sun on his face. His cell phone was tucked under the towel. He pulled it out and checked for missed calls. There was one from "MM." He called the number back.

Mindi answered on the first ring. "Hey handsome."

"Hey. What's up?"

"Nothing much. How's the surfing going?"

"How'd you know I was surfing?"

"What else would you be doing?"

"It was good. You told me the other day you really wanted to go. When are you gonna come out here so I can teach you?"

A shadow fell over Stanton. He put his hand over his eyes and saw Mindi standing there, the phone to her ear.

"Soon," she said.

He jumped to his feet. She smiled, kissed him, and put her arms around him. He looked out over the ocean as she held him. A heron dipped into the waves and came back out, slick and wet as it flew away. The ocean was alive, and it held the promise that all living things held.

That no matter what, tomorrow would always be better.

Printed in the USA
CPSIA information can be obtained
at www.ICGtesting.com
LVHW041742100324
774065LV00031B/288